THE BONE WEAVER'S ORCHARD

SARAH READ

TREPIDATIO
PUBLISHING

Trepidatio Publishing books may be ordered through booksellers or by contacting:

Trepidatio Publishing
www.trepidatio.com
or
JournalStone
www.journalstone.com

ISBN: 978-1-947654-68-6 (sc)
ISBN: 978-1-947654-69-3 (ebook)

Trepidatio rev. date: February 1, 2019

Library of Congress Control Number: 2018956782

Printed in the United States of America

Cover Art & Design: Mikio Murakami
Interior Layout: Jess Landry

Edited by Scarlett R. Algee
Proofread by Sean Leonard

THE BONE
WEAVER'S
ORCHARD

For my boys,
and for the missing one.

Thanks are first due to Jess Landry for taking on this book and giving it life, and to Scarlett Algee for saving me from my bad habits.

A thousand thanks to my mentors and those who have acted as mentors, especially Rena Mason, Danielle Kaheaku, Richard Thomas, Alec Shane, and dear Dallas Mayr.

And all my thanks to the world's best army of beta readers: Jen Koch, Regina Fontaine, Anna King, Debbie Bliemel, Torii Cannon, Awilda Baoumgren, Wendy Hammer, Kristi Heck, Troy Becker, Karen Runge, Simon Dewar, Matt Garcia, Matt Andrew, Julie C. Day, Jordan Kurella, and Kat Köhler.

A monument of thanks to my patron of the arts and coffee fairy Kathryn Grusauskas.

And thank you to my husband and sons, with special thanks to Charles—thank you for letting me borrow your name. I didn't think you were coming to claim it and I'm so very happy that you did.

DUNLEIGH ABBEY
NORTH YORKSHIRE, 1926

Charley Winslow pressed his teeth together to keep them from cracking as the car grated along the stone lane to the ancient abbey. His fresh pine tack box weighed heavily on his bony knees. The glass jars inside clinked and rang like small bells. He tried to keep them steady, imagining the terror in the hundreds of eyes inside.

You must be even colder than I am.

He pulled a yellow linen scarf from his neck, untangling it from the length of twine that suspended his numbered card. He held the scarf briefly to his nose and breathed deeply before lifting the lid of his box and tucking the cloth carefully around his specimens.

The scenery outside his window had changed from sweeping fields to dry brush and stone, windswept shrubs that seemed to want to tear themselves up from the land.

Their roots are strong. Deep. Maybe this wind will carry me away.

The great stone edifice emerged from the rock of the moor, black against the sky. At the center of the roof, a tower rose, its bell a silhouette in its carven frame. Lit windows dotted the abbey's long corridor arms, stretching across dark lawns.

They have electric lights.

His gaze traced the shape of the building by their glow. One wing remained dark, windows black and empty, so the whole of it was nearly invisible in the darkness until its shadow stretched across the car. Charley peered up at its stained bricks and shuddered.

The driver slowed the car, and the millstone wheels ground to a halt in the gravel. The man snugged his cap down tight against the wind and got out. Charley heard the crash of his trunk hitting the stones. His door sprang open, and a rush of cold stole his breath.

"Does tha need help wi' yer case?" the driver asked, reaching for the pine box.

"No!" Charley gripped the rough wood closer to his chest and slid from the seat to the drive. He swayed, unaccustomed to the sudden stillness around him. He'd been a body in motion for months— from Cairo to Algiers, to sea, through the straits, north and north again, colder and colder to Portsmouth. Then by train, north and colder, through London and York. Then in the car, north again and colder still, to these dark moors and the reaching stone arms of the Old Cross School for Boys. His body didn't know how to be still.

He tried to steady himself and felt the driver's hand on his shoulder.

"Watch tha'sen up those steps, lad. Pull the bell, an' Miss Mary will see tha'rt fed and warmed." He nudged Charley toward the tall door. The wind shrieked, plucking Charley's battered tag from the twine around his neck and carrying it off into the dark. His heart leapt as if to chase it, until he remembered he didn't need it anymore. *Don't lose your tag,* his father had said. *It's how they'll get you to the right place.*

From where he was standing, the school seemed to take up the whole sky. He couldn't even see any stars. *How can this be the right place?*

The gravel became flagstones, and the stones became stairs as the face of the old abbey towered over him. In the shelter of those rough stones, the howl of wind quieted to a distant moan.

Charley felt the cold of the stone through his shoes. He hoisted his box and imagined he could hear the enraged scurrying of a thousand chitinous legs. He squeezed it to his chest and hoped his heartbeat might calm them, that his body might somehow keep them warm in this icy wind. He pulled the bell with his teeth. The car's guttural engine idled as the driver waited to confirm that his charge had been delivered.

Charley rested his chin on the pine, caught a whiff of its bitter freshness, and wondered if the jars inside might have saved him one last breath of Cairo.

The door's hinges screamed, and a seam of light appeared in the center of its wide panel. Charley started, straightened, and knew that the hammering of his heart would only stir his charges more.

The car pulled away, digging into the gravel and vanishing into the dark. The headlamps shrank to pinpricks across the moor. Charley felt as though the lifeline was being unwound from his heart.

A lean woman in a black dress stood behind the door. Her pinched face was lit in flickering silhouette from a nearby candle. Her small eyes darted from Charley to his box, to the worn trunk on the stones behind him. "Term doesn't start for days yet," she said, holding the door as if to close it again.

"Wait—Ma'am. I don't have anywhere else to go. Or any way to get there, if I did." Charley's back was beginning to ache from the heavy box.

The woman's thin lip curled. "The village is three miles down the lane. This isn't a hotel. Someone there will take you in."

"Please, I don't know anyone in the village. I don't even know what it's called. I've just come from Cairo, where my father... He sent me away. He sent me here." Charley felt his face begin to heat. If he'd had any money, he'd have turned and walked those three miles and bought a ticket south. As many tickets south as it took to get back to his father.

The pinched woman sighed. "I guess you'd best come inside. I'll send someone for your trunk." She opened the door wide, and

Charley stepped through the stone arch into the school. The door swung shut behind him with a bang like a fortress cannon.

"Your name?" The woman in black lifted her candle from a small stand that supported a marble bust. The side of the statue's face was blackened, as if by a hundred brief encounters with the candle.

"Charley Winslow," he said.

"Wait here. I'll find where you're meant to go," she said, and left, taking the light with her.

No, you won't. Not here. He'd never felt so out of place before.

In the darkness, he felt the heaviness of stone all around him like a tomb. He felt the hollowness of the long halls, cold as a lost knife and dark as a throat.

The rustling inside his box sounded like a whisper.

CHAPTER ONE

Charley was running out of time. He climbed off the creaking school bed and gathered his jars. Tongue pressed between his teeth, he pried the lids from the twelve jars of dead specimens—glass coffins for exotic corpses. He sucked his lower lip to stop it from shaking and slid the husks into the shadowbox, held his breath as he laid them out, and slammed the empty jars against the stained floorboards.

I should break them, he thought. *Better to shatter the glass than to fill them with common damselflies.*

He closed the glass lid of the box and wrapped it in a long cream linen scarf embroidered with gold and red orchids. His thumb pressed against the ornate "SLW" stitched into the corner, the dye from the silk thread running into the weave of fibers.

Charley climbed back onto the bed, careful not to shake the thin mattress. Seven jars spanned the narrow width of the bed, survivors of the journey from the Port of Algiers. Dim light reflected dully from dozens of faceted eyes. Thin legs twitched, lifting and stabbing at fresh wet leaves and dark earth. The brassy lids, pocked with narrow holes, rang against the bars of the enameled metal foot rail as Charley leaned forward, reaching for *Pachymerium ferrugineum.*

He held his hand steady, arching each finger in succession as the centipede rippled across his knuckles. The barbs of its feet pinched in rhythm with the rain thrashing the window. The beat echoed through the empty dormitory, and Charley breathed with it, humming.

He rotated his wrist so his palm faced up, presenting a new path for the five-inch rope of legs as the centipede reached the end of his hand. The centipede circled his wrist and slid under the starched white cuff of his uniform.

Charley twisted the clasp of his cufflink and pulled it free; the fresh fabric sprang open, and the centipede scurried deeper for cover. It pinched the skin in the crease of his elbow, clinging to safety. Charley flinched and smiled. *Don't bite.*

He leaned forward, dangling his arm over the open jar. He tapped at the sleeve by his elbow and felt the stiff segments curl, sacrificing grip to form a shield. With another tap, the pinching grasp slid from the fine hairs of his arm and the long rust-colored strand tumbled into the jar.

Charley replaced the lid and screwed it down, forcing the worn threads of the lid to align with the jar's rim. He pulled a magnifying glass from its tooled case and examined his specimen. It uncoiled and raced around the perimeter of the jar, head and tail nearly touching, counting away the vanishing seconds with its many legs.

Charley grabbed for the other jars, crammed the lids in place, and lined them up in his tack box.

A deep growl cut through the patter of rain against the window. Charley pressed his forehead to the cool glass, peering down through the squall to the row of cars idling in front of the school— sleek black cars with oiled cloth tops that shed the rain, so unlike the dust-colored trucks of the military camp. Footfalls echoed up the stairway, sweeping through the halls. The air warmed with the heat of moving bodies, carrying the scent of rain-wet wool and pine boxes dragged across floors. Voices slid down polished floorboards, a wordless hum as the school came awake.

Across the soggy lawn, the boards nailed over the windows of the abandoned East Wing darkened, soaked in the driving rain. The wind pulled at the boards, slamming the loose ones against the grey flaking stone with cracks that echoed over the empty lawns.

Charley turned as footsteps sounded behind him, his fog mask left on the glass.

A tall boy walked into the room, his dark hair longer than was allowed, brushing his stiff white collar. He punched a button on the wall, and the electric sconce lights flickered awake. Charley flinched at the sudden bright light—so much more severe than candle or campfire, sharper than soft lanterns.

The boy dragged his trunk to the foot of Charley's bed and sat down on the mattress; the metal joints screeched. He pried his shoes off, shaking muddy water from them.

"When they're dry, polish them," he said. He flashed straight white teeth, the brightest thing in the room. "You know how this works, yeah? You work for me this term. Thank you for keeping my bed warm. You look like you were well settled."

"Yes, sir," Charley said, gathering his tack box and trunk and dragging them to another bed. His father had warned him of this, of older boys bossing the younger ones. *It's much like the military, Charles. You'll recognize it. Do your duty and you'll be fine.* He'd pulled leaves from Charley's hair then. Told him he'd have to learn to dress smartly.

"How were you here before me? I'm always the first to arrive." The boy had begun unpacking his trunk, stacking magazines on the nightstand, slipping some under the mattress.

"My father had to send me early." Charley swallowed. "I've been here a few days."

"First year, yeah?" asked the boy, draping his jacket over the foot rail. "You know what's expected of you, then?"

"Yes."

"Sir."

"Yes, sir."

"I'm Malcolm Amos. Head boy." He extended long tapered fingers, thumb tip curving back like a lily petal.

"Charley Winslow."

Charley grasped the hand, the fingers enveloping his before slipping away as Malcolm turned to another boy entering the room. Malcolm crossed the room in two wide strides and embraced the boy. They laughed, speaking too quickly with their lilting accents for Charley to understand. The driver who'd brought him from the station insisted Yorkshire was English. Charley supposed it was, but felt it might as well not be.

Two more boys walked in. Charley stepped back and sat on the edge of his new bed, eyes askance on the window and the free, open air beyond it. The room felt smaller every moment.

A small boy pushed through the forest of legs, his pine box perched slipping on his round hip, arm pulled back to the trunk behind him. He slid his box down his leg to the floor and kicked it under the bed next to Charley's. The contents of the small box rattled, its corners gouging the flaking floorboards.

"Hello," the boy said. "Are you in my year?"

"First?"

"Yeah. Ethan Bowles. Nice to meet you." Ethan removed his felt cap, trying to mold the damp wool back into shape. His coarse yellow hair sprang up like fern tines.

"Charley Winslow."

"Where are you from, Charley? I can tell it isn't Yorkshire."

"Nowhere, really," Charley said. The boy had a southern accent himself. London, Charley supposed, or maybe Oxford. He didn't get the chance to ask.

"Ah. Here for some institutionalized child-minding, then. Not 'the family legacy'. That's me as well." Bowles looked down, his fingernails raised to his lips. His hands were dimpled but calloused, his fingernails black against pale pink cuticles. He nodded to the pin on Charley's lapel. "Your dad in Cairo?"

"Yes. I just came from there. He put me on a boat as soon as the riots started."

Bowles' fair eyebrows rose. "He had you there with him?"

"Wasn't anywhere else to go."

"You mean apart from our fine school." Bowles tugged at a rusted claw of bedspring poking from the side of his mattress.

The corner of Charley's mouth twitched.

"If you come here, either your dad is rich, or he's an officer. Best if it's both, though. Is it both?"

Charley shook his head.

The cluster of older boys around Malcolm had grown. His fingers raised above their heads in wild gesture, laughter bouncing off the stone walls. The laughter soured, turned to gasps.

"Jesus, what the hell?" An older boy jumped, arms flung back. He lunged, leg kicking forward. His foot came down, cracking against the floorboards. Something popped.

"What was that?" The boys closed their circle around a spot on the floor.

"It's a monster," one said, leaning in, then pulling back.

"Do you think there are more of them?"

"Never seen one like that before."

"Bet it came from the East Wing."

The hair on Charley's neck rose. Head spinning, he leapt from the bed and pushed his face into the ring of boys. It was his giant *Palystes superciliosus*, her eight long legs broken, tucked into her crushed abdomen. Her chelicerae twitched, reaching, and then stilled.

Charley shouldered his way into the ring and scooped her up. Tears spilled over his cheeks as a low moan pulled from his lungs.

The ring of boys expanded backward.

Charley forced himself to breathe. He stood. Shaking, he walked to his tack box and set the dead spider on the lid. He spun to the silent arc of boys, locked eyes with the stomper. Charley flew at him, hands outstretched, coated in slick yellow juice. He clawed at the chest of the boy, raking at every part he could reach.

Hands grasped his arms, pulling him back, dragging him away. A shoulder pressed against his face as an arm circled his throat.

"What is going on here? Amos, explain," a low voice bellowed from the doorway.

The hands holding Charley fell away, the arm slithering from his throat as Malcolm straightened and stepped forward.

"Master Brown, I believe Mullins has accidentally…broken something of Winslow's."

"Winslow, come here, boy."

Charley tensed his muscles, trying to smother the quaking in his legs as he walked to the broad figure enveloped in folds of black robes.

A dark beard, streaked with silver, hung from the end of the sagging face. Yellow-rimmed eyes peered down through the thicket of whiskers at Charley's bowed head.

"Explain yourself," Master Brown said.

"I'm sorry, sir. Mullins accidentally destroyed one of my…science specimens. I'm afraid I lost my temper."

"And what sort of specimens did you feel it was necessary to bring with you to school?"

Charley swept his gaze over the faces turned to him. He swallowed. He walked to his tack box. Reaching under the sheet, he felt *Palystes'* jar on its side, the lid gaping where it hadn't screwed down. He pushed the jar away and pulled out a thin shadowbox. Inside, rows of dry beetles were pinned to a burlap backcloth. Scrawled labels under each of the variously sized and colored insects gave the scientific name, location, and date of capture.

He handed the case to the housemaster. "Entomology, sir. I enjoy the study of insects."

Master Brown pulled a pair of spectacles from the bramble atop his head and peered down his cratered nose at the samples. Light from the hall flashed off the iridescent wings, casting green and gold specters across his face.

"I take it he mistook one for vermin? An easy enough mistake to make, as that's what they are." Charley dropped his gaze to the man's scuffed shoes. "See to it your samples are kept away in future, and that your temper remains under your control at all times. Your outburst has earned you five strikes. Amos," he handed the box back to Charley and turned to the older boy, "please see it done." He turned and stalked away in a cloud of black cloth and moth dust.

Charley set the shadowbox on his bed. He turned to the boys, his housemates all watching, saying nothing. Malcolm held a long cane in his hand like an extension of his willowy arm. It trembled slightly, as if caught in a breeze. Bowles' eyes were wide, pale and watery, the skin around them translucent pink against his blanched face.

"Take down your trousers, turn around, and put your hands on the bedrail," Malcolm said. Charley obeyed, feeling the eyes of the boys roll over his exposed skin. The heat rising to his face made his eyes burn.

The first strike didn't hurt until the cane was at its apex again, pain blossoming just as the second impact lanced across the soft skin of his thighs. An ache, deep and muscular, sharpened to a sting as welts formed atop bruises.

By the fourth swing, Charley howled. The corridors of the South Wing fell silent. His screams were an anthem, signifying the opening of the term.

When it was over, he pulled himself onto the bed, dragging his trousers dangling from his feet and curling his arm around the shadowbox. He buried his face in the crisp, threadbare blanket. Boys chuckled, turning to their own business.

Through the thunder of blood in his ears, Charley heard the porcelain ring of the ewer against the basin. Bowles set a cup of water on the table between their beds.

A bell rang through the school and the boys filed from the room, punching out the gold glow of light, merging into a flowing corridor that poured down the stairs to the old chapel ballroom for dinner.

Charley stayed on his bed. He turned to face his tack box. The light from the window had faded to almost nothing, but he could see the crumpled silhouette of *Palystes*. He hummed, squeezing the tune through his tight throat. The song was an old one, sung under palm fronds and in tents across the desert, on camels' backs and under the decks of steamships far from home. He should have set her loose on the coast to hunt lizards and lay eggs, not brought her to this dark, wet cloud of a moor.

He sang to her as he stood, fixing his trousers in place. In the fading, rain-filtered light, he saw seven spattered pairs of shoes tossed by his bedside, from Bowles' short and wide to the long sweeping soles of Malcolm's, to Sean Mullins', the stomper, fouled with yellow guts. A stack of folded rags sat next to the pile.

Charley went to his tack box and removed a jar. Inside it, two wolf spiders brawled. He unscrewed the lid and tipped one of the hairy creatures into his palm, then slipped it between the rumpled sheets of Sean's bed.

* * *

Nostrils burning with the scent of polish, Charley feigned sleep as the boys returned to the dormitory. They tromped across the old boards, laughing and slamming trunk lids, changing into their nightclothes.

Through his cracked eyelids, Charley watched Bowles lean over him, then turn to his own bed. The boy bent, reached under his bed into his pine box, pulled something out, and set it on the bed table they shared. It thudded against the wood tabletop and sparkled in the light from the hall. Spines of glass, clear crystal towers, rose from a curved matrix of jumbled grey and white stone. Light refracted through its angles, casting small bright slivers across the wall. Bowles ran his fingers over its edges, smoothing the crystal faces. Then he, too, climbed into bed and pulled the stiff blanket over himself.

Charley realized he'd opened his eyes when he saw Bowles looking at him. Bowles' dirty fingernails were in his mouth again. His pale eyes sparkled in the shadow across his face, and then the sparkle winked out. Bowles' breathing evened.

On the floor between the rows of beds, the second-form boys rattled marbles. Sean Mullins exploited the grooves in the wooden planks, collecting orbs from the others, laughing off their vows for vengeance. They carried on until the starched Matron Grace rang a bell in the hall, and the sounds throughout the school faded into the settling creak of the old building walls, the groan of old wood and stone rippling down from the attics through the corridors, tumbling down the stairs, silenced at the bottom.

* * *

Moonlight from the narrow window cast unfamiliar shadows that slid unexpectedly along the walls. The walls groaned and gurgled. The boys in their beds sighed, moaned, and snorted in their sleep. Every hour, the tapping heels of the master on night duty passed through the hall, the light from his lamp falling across the rows of beds, casting rounded shadows high on the far wall. The wind outside threw rain at the window, slacking to a quiet, steady drum, then hurling it like ballast. The trees in the arbor rustled and creaked.

Charley rolled in his sheets. He conjured memories of the utter silence of the desert, heat rising from the sun-warmed sand to soak through his bedroll and into his bones, tired from hiking dunes and chasing scorpions.

The hiss of wind-blown sand against oiled tent canvas shattered as words formed in the whispers, grated out of a raw throat, guttural and low. A soft writhing of slow-moving feet scraped across the floor. A board creaked under uneven weight.

Charley lay still. He forced himself to breathe more deeply and evenly, raising and lowering his chest in time with the sleeping figures around him.

Something soft brushed against the doorframe. A bent shape stood outlined against the dim light of the hallway. It lumbered into the room as if dragging something behind it. It paused by each bed, leaning over, peering into the sleeping faces of the boys, whispering too quietly for Charley to hear, a rapid cadence of lisping breath. The figure laughed as it leaned over Bowles, its voice dry as wasp wings.

Charley relaxed his eyes, relaxed his jaw and face, let it all fall slack, and focused on breathing. The figure didn't look like any of the masters he'd met. The steps shuffled closer.

A hot, moist cloud of breath painted his cheek. He smelled dust and dead teeth.

"So small, the new ones, so little to be had." It turned from him, hobbled to the center of the room, and stopped.

There was a sharp pop, and a crunch, and another, and again. The scuffing feet scraped across the floor.

Charley watched the figure move from the room and turn into

the hall, heard the shuffles retreat down the corridor. He pulled in a shaking breath and wiped the foul condensation from his cheek. He sat up, panting, watching shadows slip along the walls.

The tap-tap and swaying light of the patrolling master passed down the hall again, the glow of the oily wick overwhelming his pupils. Charley squeezed his eyes shut and pulled the blanket over his face. He counted the master's steps, counted the seconds till the master passed again, kept his eyes squeezed shut, and, forgetting to open them again, he slept.

* * *

The bell that woke him roused a general moan along the corridor. Boys slid from their beds into the grey morning, bare feet flinching back from the cold boards. Sean Mullins leapt from bed, then fell back, howling, clutching his feet. A trickle of blood ran between his fingers.

Strewn across the floor were Sean's marbles, some crushed to shards, others to powder, broken glass seeded across the central lane of the room.

Sean pulled splinters of glass from his foot. As each piece clattered to the floor, faces turned to Charley. His eyes widened and he shook his head, afraid to speak. The heads turned, slowly, back to Sean's foot, sparkling red with bloody glass.

CHAPTER TWO

Charley tucked his face inside his grey wool scarf. The wind blew droplets of rain from the tree leaves, tapping against the brim of his cap, startling him from a half-sleep. The ground oozed, saturated by autumn showers. Pools of standing water speckled the grounds, preventing morning drills from occupying the crowd of boys.

Charley stood beneath an elm tree, his nose inches from the trunk, staring deep into the folds of bark. He turned to the sound of squishing footsteps behind him.

Bowles approached, his face pink, his chin quivering above his scarf, hands thrust deep in his pockets. "Are you hiding here?" he asked, wiping his running nose against his scarf.

"Not really, no. I'm just looking for what things live in this tree," Charley said. He turned back to the rough grey bark.

"Bugs?"

"Yeah."

"Any good ones?" Bowles leaned toward the tree.

Charley turned back to the boy, searching his face for the hidden half-smile of mockery, but saw only raw pink cheeks and watery eyes. "Not really. That was a neat rock you brought out last night. Is that your thing, rocks?"

Bowles' eyes lit. "Yeah, it is. I brought a few my father sent from his tours in Africa. I was hoping to find more here. Want to look with me? I saw from Master Culvert's window that they're turning over a new garden on the north end, on the east side. Bound to be bugs and rocks in that patch."

Charley nodded, and they left the shelter of the tree. They walked around the tip of the South Wing, hugging the stone wall, their drab woolens merging with the shade. The dorm hall windows reflected grey light from the low, damp sky. As they rounded the tip of the East Wing, they came across twenty square meters of freshly turned earth, lumpy and wet from rain. A shovel and pick stuck out of the ground along its neat edge.

Charley and Bowles walked to the side of the patch and knelt in the wet grass, soaking the knees of their trousers. The earth smelled of torn green roots, dark and loamy, refreshing after the close walls of the school.

Waterlogged worms floated in muddy puddles, flooded from their tunnels. "Not going to be many bugs till this dries up a bit," Charley said. "There's a pile of rocks over there, though."

They walked around the patch to the pile of stones scattered around an overturned wheelbarrow. Bowles sat and pawed at the pile, tossing aside grey lumps, dismissing them as common local stone, nothing special.

"What was that rock last night—the one with all the crystals?" Charley asked.

"Oh, that's special. It's a geode. Looks like plain rock on the outside, but when you break it open, it's full of crystals."

"So how can you tell when a plain rock is full of crystals?"

"That's the trick, isn't it? You learn to tell. To see." Bowles squinted at a hunk of rock before dropping it back into the mud.

Charley gazed up at the school. Windows along the North Wing were propped open, airing the classrooms between lessons, taking advantage of the September breezes before October froze the wind in place. The East Wing stretched out at a right angle, dark stains running down from boarded and broken windows. Warped planks, sprung free from their nails, dangled from the shutters. Tattered bits of curtains fluttered in breezes blown through broken panes, dancing in and out of view. Charley squinted at the shifting shapes.

"Look at this one," said Bowles, holding up a lump of dark rock.

Charley leaned over it. "What am I seeing?"

"Igneous rock. Not from here—probably from Wales."

"How'd it get here, then?" Charley took the rock from Bowles and held it close to his eye, squinting for a clue written on its rough surface.

"Might have been blasted here in a volcanic eruption. Or dragged here by a glacier. Or someone brought it. Mystery." Bowles took the rock back, dropped it into his pocket and resumed digging.

"Is that one full of crystals?"

Bowles smiled. "No, not this one."

"Have you ever dug up a bone?" Charley pulled a small spade from the earth and began to dig. He understood, now, why Bowles' fingernails were so dirty.

"Oh, yeah—lots of times."

"Like fossils?" Charley asked.

"Only once. A fossil bone is really just a rock. Usually I find rabbit or mouse bones. Probably buried by foxes. Not old bones."

"How can you tell how old a bone is?" Every bone Charley had ever seen had seemed like stone, anyway. *We have stones inside of us instead of crystals. Why not wear our bones on the outside, like insects? To keep us safer. Except from stompers.* He felt the drop of grief in his gut again.

"By how deep it is in the ground, usually. The deeper you go, the older it is." Bowles hadn't noticed Charley's thoughts wandering away from the dirt patch.

"Bones sink?" Charley asked.

"No. New dirt settles on top of it. Layers and layers, a tiny bit at a time."

"So if there was a bone from four hundred years ago, way back when this was a church, how deep would it be?"

"Probably only a dozen centimeters. It's a slow process, and it depends a lot on climate and weather. It's not really accurate over such a short period."

"Short?" Charley felt that the last few days had been long enough to bury the entire school.

"Short for geology, yeah. Besides, it doesn't work so well with human bones." Bowles' arms were elbow-deep in a hole that filled slowly with leeching groundwater. It smelled of soaking rot.

"Why not?"

"Because we bury the dead. Dig holes. When you find a human bone in the ground, it's usually because someone put it there."

Charley slowed his digging. "The old abbey probably had graves all around it. All over these grounds."

Bowles slowed, too. "Yeah. I suppose it probably did."

"Did the earls move them all, do you think?"

"I don't think you're allowed to."

Their eyes raked over the soil at their feet.

"Well, I wouldn't want my garden full of bodies." Charley dropped his shovel.

"And I wouldn't want my grave stomped over by a bunch of noisy asses." Bowles nodded toward the distant cricket game.

Charley cracked a grin. "No wonder the halls are full of ghosts. Who could sleep through that?"

"Halls are a racket, too. Any ghost wants rest around here probably stays in the East Wing. That's where I'd go for a good nap."

"Has anyone ever gone in there?" Charley's gaze wandered back to the stained stone face of the East Wing.

"Not for years. It's falling apart, they say. One boy went in through a window once and broke both his legs. No one ever saw him again. Said he was sent home to die. That's when they boarded it all up. Every boy that's tried since gets the lashing of the century. No one's tried in a while, that I've heard."

"How do you know all this?"

"My cousin's been through. He took his exams last May." Bowles rubbed at the mud that clung to his arms.

Charley stared up at the row of windows, the broken boards smiling down like rotted teeth. "I bet it is quiet there. I could use a nap." They were empty, the tattered cloth strips settled back, out of sight. "Do you think they'll ever fix it up? Have classes there?"

"My cousin said he asked the headmaster once. He told him they tried, but that it wasn't safe." Bowles scraped his fingernails over the surface of a pale stone. "The earl shut it up. Something about a fire weakening the stone. The earl's wife and her maid died there when a wall collapsed, and there wasn't enough money left with the estate to save that part. They bricked over the entrances and left it."

"It seems such a waste."

Bowles smiled. "It gives the ghosts a place to stay." He straightened, dropping more rocks into his blazer pockets. "Not bad for a mud pile," he said, reaching into his pockets and wrapping his earthy fingers around the treasures.

Charley couldn't see anything special about the rocks Bowles had chosen, but he supposed most people didn't see anything special about his spiders, either.

They walked back around the East Wing, Charley sloshing through puddles, soaking his shoes as he stared up at the crumbling stone ledges, dwelling on thoughts of trapped ghosts.

"Was it you that crushed Sean's marbles?" Bowles startled him from his thoughts.

Charley's stomach dropped at the memory of Malcolm plucking glass from Sean's foot. "No! I swear I didn't. I saw a man in the room last night. He did it. He was angry, muttering. Dressed in rags, and he had a bad limp. I don't know him. He must be one of the staff."

Bowles stared at Charley, his mouth agape. "You're fooling."

"No, I'm not. He was creepy."

"You saw the ragged man."

"Who is he?"

"My cousin said he's a ghost. It's bad luck to see him."

Charley frowned. "A ghost couldn't break marbles. He's probably a cleaner. Must have been furious over the mess."

Bowles shrugged a shoulder. The stones in his pocket rattled.

"That's the story, is all. You see him—means you're gonna die."

In the shadows at the juncture of the East and South Wings, a crowd of senior boys handed around wisping cigarettes, blowing smoky laughs.

"Oik," one shouted. He strode up to Bowles and slapped the cap from his head and yanked at his arms. "No hands in your pockets. It's a rule. Go stand by the wall."

Bowles didn't move; his dirty hands splayed in front of him. The older boy shoved him against the wall, drew his fist back and swung it around, straight into Bowles' middle. Bowles grunted.

The boy clutched his fist and screamed, bending over around his hands.

"What the hell is wrong with you?" another asked.

The boy coughed smoke, caught his breath. "He's got something in his pockets," he said, holding up his hand. The knuckles swelled, darkening.

The boys surrounded Bowles, grabbed his arms and reached into his pockets. They drew out handfuls of rocks. They laughed, frowning down at Bowles' bowed head.

"What's this? Weights to keep your hollow head from floating you away?" They laughed again.

"Start running, oik," said one.

Bowles' eyes grew wider. Charley grabbed his hand and pulled, dragging him, racing across the lawn. Rocks sailed past their heads, splashing in puddles at their feet. Charley felt the hot, stinging swipe of a rock graze his arm.

Crack. Bowles fell, unmoving, face-down in a puddle. Charley stopped and turned. The older boys scattered and fled around the arm of the East Wing.

Blood ran from the back of Bowles' head, clumping his straw hair.

Charley hauled at the shoulder of Bowles' jacket, turning him to his side, pulling his face from the puddle. He was breathing, but his mouth hung slack, his eyes dull slits in his pale face.

"Help!" Charley called across the lawn.

Faces appeared around the corner of the South Wing, and disappeared.

Bowles groaned, his hands waving aimlessly in the air. His eyelids fluttered. Charley felt warm blood soaking the leg of his trousers where Bowles' head rested.

The bright white triangle of the matron's apron advanced across the grass, her cloak billowing behind her as she ran. Master Brown followed, his square cap askew.

"Ooh," Bowles moaned, reaching for his head, trying to lift himself.

Matron Grace dropped to the grass next to him. She grasped his shoulders and pulled him forward, staring into his face. His head lolled to the side, spilling a trickle of blood across her knee. She pried at his eyelids, saw the blood in his hair, and brushed the sticky strands aside, inspecting the wound.

"This will need stitches," she said. "Both of you, help me carry him."

Master Brown looked down at Charley, his eyebrows low. "You're Charley Winslow," he said, pressing a thick hand against the pocket of his waistcoat.

"Yes, sir," Charley said. The master's eyes were as dark as the low clouds, glaring down at him.

"Take him under the arms," the matron said. She removed Bowles' scarf and pressed it against the back of his head. He whimpered.

Charley and the master each took an arm, navigating the soggy terrain with Bowles' toes dragging in the wet grass between them. The matron followed, holding the scarf to his bloody scalp. The pale grey wool darkened under her hand.

They faltered up the flagstone steps and into the school, dripping muddy water and blood across the checkered tiles of the entry hall. They turned into the surgery and set Bowles in a large leather chair by the hearth.

"Hold this," Matron Grace said, and Charley took hold of the scarf, pressing it against Bowles' scalp.

The matron dashed around the room, set a kettle to boil on a hotplate, and collected bottles and a small wooden box banded in brass. She laid them out on a tray and poured steaming water into a basin before pulling a handful of thin towels from the cupboard.

Dragging a stool to the side of Bowles' chair, she set her tray on a small table. She reached up and peeled the scarf away slowly and set it aside, its folds printed with blood, the fibers meshed, dark and sticky.

A furrow of flesh folded back from Bowles' skull, gold hair sticking in the wound. Matron Grace dipped a cloth in the steaming water and sponged at the mess. She rinsed and sponged; the water in the basin turned bright red.

Charley jumped up. He took the basin and poured the red water into the drain, refilled the bowl from the steaming kettle, and set more to boil.

"Thank you," the matron said. She took sharp scissors and cut away clumps of Bowles' golden hair, setting them on a cloth spread across her lap. She wiped and cut until the wound was clear and clean. She folded the thatch of bloody straw into the towel in her lap. Master Brown took it from her and placed it in the cabinet.

"Will you need any further assistance, Grace?" he asked.

"No, Master Brown. Charley will assist me, thank you." She smiled at Charley.

Master Brown left the room, pulling the heavy wooden door closed behind him.

Matron Grace opened the case and pulled out a long needle and a spool of black cord. She threaded the needle and tied a knot, pulling it tight with her teeth.

"Hold him," she said.

Charley grasped Bowles' wrists, but met no resistance. The hands were limp, the boy's head bowed forward, unmoving.

Matron Grace smoothed the flap of skin in place, spreading it over the white layer of bone. She pressed it down. Blood seeped up around the pressure of her fingers. She slipped the needle through the edge of the flap, looped the thread around, and slid it in again.

Her fingertips shone red. "Are you going to tell me what happened?"

"Some older boys were throwing stones," Charley said.

"At you? On purpose?"

"Yes, ma'am."

"You should report it to the headmaster." Grace paused and rinsed her hands in the red water.

"I don't know their names. I barely saw their faces."

"Well. If there's any more trouble, try to remember." She dried her hands on her white apron, leaving prints of blossom-pink blood.

"Yes, ma'am."

"Call me Grace."

Bowles' eyelids fluttered, the round shapes rolling beneath them. He panted, teeth grinding together, a whine building in his throat. His eyes popped open, his mouth growing round and wide.

Charley gripped his wrists tighter. "It's not too bad," he said, "You'll have a great scar, though. Want to see something?" Bowles blinked and clamped his jaw tight.

Charley bent, lifting the leg of his trousers. He released the clip of the special garter that held his left sock in place, pulled down the cuff of his stocking, and turned his leg. His calf rippled, deep red crevices capped with white mounds of scar tissue.

Matron Grace leaned from behind Bowles. "Is that a burn?" she asked, turning back to her work.

"No," Charley said, "spider bite. I was camping with my father's regiment. It had crawled into my boot, and I put my leg in. Our guide sucked out some of the poison, but my skin kept turning black, and they had to cut away bits of it to keep it from spreading."

Bowles pulled away from the matron, drawing her thread taut. He leaned over the edge of the chair and vomited.

Charley leapt to his feet. He grabbed a clean basin from the cupboard and handed it to Bowles.

"Sorry, I…" Charley said.

"I don't think it was that," the matron said, handing Bowles a damp cloth. "He has a concussion."

Bowles coughed and spluttered into the basin. Matron Grace leaned over him, finishing her last few stitches and tying a knot close to Bowles' scalp. She snipped the cord and sponged away the blood. She handed Bowles a small cup filled with a milky grey liquid from one of her dark glass bottles. Bowles took the cup and choked down the medicine.

"Charley, would you get Bowles' night things? He'll need to stay in the infirmary tonight where I can keep an eye on him. And take these upstairs for him, if you would." She handed him Bowles' damp jacket, blood-stained scarf, and muddy shoes.

"Yes, Matron," Charley said. He hurried down the hall to the staircase and climbed to the second level, turning into the South Wing. He passed the row of open dormitory doors, each filled with eight boys of mixed ages, laughter tumbling out and down the hall. His dorm went silent as he entered, and they all turned to him: standing in the doorway, covered in blood.

Charley laid Bowles' things on his bed, leaned to his trunk, opened it, and pulled out the crumpled nightclothes. He hurried from the room.

Instead of turning to the grand staircase, he ran to the end of the hall, past the remaining dorms and closet, to the servants' stairs. Free from the exposure of electric lights, he stepped down around the curving staircase to the back hall. He crept through the still, dark corridor, past the kitchens and dining hall to the infirmary.

Bowles was stretched out atop the sheets of a narrow bed, unconscious. Matron Grace leaned over him, pulling at the wound on his head, pressing the skin together, aligning the stitches. Charley walked up behind her. She started and turned, clutching at her bloody apron.

She let out a breath that smelled of peppermint. "Thank you, Charley." She took the clothes from him.

"Will the damage be permanent?" Charley asked, digging dried blood from under his nails.

"I don't believe so," she said, "but I'll know more in the morning. He may be here for a few days."

Charley nodded.

"Thank you for your help, Charley. I've informed the headmaster that Bowles will be out of classes. Please let your head boy know, so no one will believe him missing."

"Yes, Matron."

She reached her hand out to shake his. When he grasped it, she pulled his wrist over, examining a streak of blood on his forearm.

34

"Are you hurt too, Charley? Why didn't you say?"

"I'm fine. A rock grazed me, but it doesn't hurt."

The matron pressed it with her thumbs, spreading the cut. It filled with fresh blood. Charley hissed, drawing his arm back.

"I'm sorry, Charley, but I need to see how deep it goes."

"It's not deep. It just stings a bit."

She reached for his arm again, pressing the wound. He stifled a whimper.

"I think I'd better stitch this, Charley, just to be safe."

Charley pressed his lips together, remembering the long needle and the thick cord. "Okay," he said.

She led him to the leather chair. He smelled vinegar where it had been wiped clean, but felt a tarry spot against his neck that had been missed.

She prepared her tray, laying out a cloth, bandages, a small bottle of clear liquid, and her needle and thread. She dabbed the cut with liquid from the bottle. A feeling like fire spread up his arm. He bit his lips closed, humming.

She bent over his arm.

He watched the early moon through the window, at the long clouds blowing across it. The matron's wispy curls cut crescents against its light, bobbing as she tugged at the cord.

When she was finished, she brought him a cup of tea, and wrapped his arm in a bandage while he sipped it. "You're a very brave patient, Charley."

"Getting sewn together isn't as bad as having pieces cut off," he said.

She raised her eyebrows. "No, I don't suppose it is. Now run along and get some rest. You can visit your friend in the morning."

Charley smiled and walked from the room. He paused in the entry hall, leaning against the carved wood banister of the grand staircase. Rows of marble busts lined the wall leading to the South Wing, faces of ancient earls, each one to the last, the founder of the school. The final bust was the sagging face of Headmaster Byrne. Charley walked past the faces. The dinner bell rang. A rising din of hungry boys sounded overhead. His stomach churned uneasily at the thought of Malcolm's questions, the boys' teasing. He wasn't hungry. He thought he might be sick instead.

Charley hurried for the front doors, pushing against one, slipping out into the night.

The grounds had filled with fog. It drifted over the damp earth, collecting in swirling pools in the low places.

Charley walked around the end of the South Wing. He bent low over the ground, running his feet over the grass as he walked. He kicked a rock from a puddle, picked it up, and put it in his pocket. He combed the grass all around, retracing his steps from that morning, picking up every rock he found, just in case. He didn't know if they were the right kind of rock. He wished he'd looked more closely when Bowles had shown him before.

He heard a splash through the fog, a clang of metal. He followed the sounds. A figure emerged from the mist, bent over a shovel, turning the earth, expanding the long deep patch of mud.

The man straightened, stretching his back, and saw Charley. "Ey up," he said. "Shouldn't tha be inside at tea?"

"Hello," Charley said. "Who are you?"

The man wiped mud from his hands to his trousers. "Samuel Forster. I'm the gardener here." He extended a hand, dark with dirt.

"Charley." He grasped the hand; grains of earth clung to his palm. "Is this a new flowerbed?"

"Vegetables, I'm afraid. I expect tha'll be seeing a lot o' turnips next term." The man smiled, white teeth shining from his dirty face. Some of the dirt fell away from the lines around his mouth. "What brings tha to th' gardens at tea time? There's nowt fit to eat out here this time of year but apples."

Charley held out a handful of rocks. "My friend was interested in these rocks. I came to collect them for him. He dropped them when…earlier."

The gardener nodded. He tugged at the whiskers on his chin. "I saw Crey an' his gang run past my greenhouse this afternoon. Mun been quite a spot o' trouble to send them runnin' like that."

Charley nodded, afraid to say too much. "Anyway, if you see more rocks like this one, could you set them aside there?" He pointed off through the fog, where the upturned wheelbarrow lay. "I'd like to take them to him. As many as I can find."

"Aye, I can do that. Has tha been out east, beyond the old wing?"

"No," Charley said. He shivered. The fog clung to his clothes, collecting into icy droplets.

"That's where I take th' rocks I dig up, the ones I don't use for walls and such. I've no use for those. Your friend might like to check there."

"Yes, I think he would. Thank you, sir."

"No 'sir'. Just Sam. I'm no master here. Which is good for thee— bein' out o' bounds and all. Best get back inside before they mark tha's missing." He raised his eyebrows and nodded back toward the school.

Charley smiled and turned back. A flicker of light through a broken board caught his eye, in a low window of the East Wing. He turned to the gardener, but he'd vanished into the fog. When Charley turned again, the light had gone.

* * *

Charley piled the rocks into Bowles' tack box, which was already half-full of other mineral specimens.

He changed into his nightclothes. When he pulled his shirt down over his face, Malcolm was in front of him.

"Where's Bowles?" he asked.

Charley blanched. He'd forgotten to carry the matron's message. "He was hurt this afternoon and needed stitches. Matron's got him in the infirmary."

"Hurt how?"

Charley pinched his lips together. He dared not imagine how the rock-throwers might retaliate if he tattled. He didn't know if Malcolm counted the boys among his friends.

Malcolm nodded slowly, his features steely. "Fine, then." He walked back to his own bed.

The night master had already begun his rounds, tonight one who walked with a heavy foot, thunking down the hall. He whipped the beam of light abruptly over each boy's face.

Charley lay down and turned toward the wall, facing the dark window. He thought of huge volcanoes blasting chunks of rock hundreds of miles. Of icy glaciers. Of prehistoric sling-wielding warriors carrying packs of rocks into tribal battles. He counted the thunks of the master's route two more times, listening to the night sounds of his housemates. He drifted into sleep.

He woke to the sound of something dragging. Again, hoarse whispers. Rustling behind him. A muffled clang. Something scraped across the floorboards. Heavy breathing blew through a constant stream of whispers. A long scrape and a thump. A dry laugh. The shuffling moved through the room, circling Charley's bed. Floorboards creaked.

Charley slowly pulled the blanket over part of his face, burying his cheek in the splintery down of his pillow, praying his trembling wouldn't cause the bedsprings to squeak. *It can't be a ghost, and luck is a myth. But Bowles...*

Silence. Then a long sigh, a clink of glass. Charley squeezed his eyes shut.

The shuffling moved to the center of the room. A rapid staccato of shattering glass, a shrieking laugh, and the high screams of startled students filled the room. The dragging steps pushed through the broken shards, out of the room, and down the corridor, a rapid skipping halt as it hurried away.

Blankets flew back as boys called out. Charley sat up, looking around the room, dizzy from holding his breath and tensing his shoulders.

Loud, heavy steps thundered down the hall. A beam of light cut through the room.

"What's going on in here? Why are you all awake?" Master Brown walked into the room. His shoes crunched across the floor. He shone his light at his feet. It glittered across the floorboards, brass discs scattered about like ancient mirrors. The floor writhed, rushing from the light, skittering under beds, into shadows.

Master Brown shouted and leaped back, dashing the light across the floor.

Sean screamed and pointed.

A giant beetle, its hooked mandibles flailing, trundled over broken shards of glass, scaling the master's shoe. The master shook his foot in the air, hopping back toward the door. He slammed his fist into the button. Yellow light flickered and filled the room. Boys buried their faces in blankets.

"What the devil is going on here?" the master screamed.

The floor sparkled with broken jars and kaleidoscope eyes, shining wings and carapaces.

Boys stood on their beds, shouting. The matron arrived at the doorway, her crisp apron thrown over a flowing night dress, her yellow hair falling wild around her shoulders. She darted down the hall to the closet and returned with a broom.

"Be careful," Charley wailed as she swept the mass back toward the wall. Insects tumbled through the shifting layers of glass.

She cleared a path to the back of the room and handed the broom to Charley.

"You will clean this at once," Master Brown said.

"I swear I didn't—"

"You and these insects have caused nothing but trouble since the start of term." Master Brown's face remained red behind his shaking whiskers.

"It wasn't me! It was a man in grey rags. He has a limp, and he's been coming in here and breaking things."

They all stared in silence at Charley. The matron's face paled to the color of her apron.

"Telling tall tales will *not* improve your situation," Brown said. Master and matron exchanged a glance; then Matron Grace motioned the boys forward.

"Boys, follow me to the infirmary. You'll spend the rest of the night there."

They filed into the narrow, cleared path and hurried from the room like ants following a pheromone trail, laughing, shooting glances over their shoulders at Charley. Master Brown thunked over to him.

"You will clean this room, you will destroy those horrible creatures, and you will report to the headmaster's office, where you will be punished." He turned from the room, following the line of boys. Charley heard him bellow down the hall at other dormitories, ordering them to return to their beds.

Charley leaned the broom against his bed and crouched down to the pile of debris. Shards of glass and crumpled chitin rolled in dust, spilled across the floor. Charley plucked a few living beetles from the rubble and dropped them into the empty water basin. Most of the living bugs had already scattered, scrambling away into the dark recesses of the room.

Charley fetched his shadowbox and pulled the embroidered linen scarf from it, winding the scarf around his neck and tucking it into his shirt, breathing in the smell of it. He pulled the dead from the pile and placed them in the box, alongside those that had never made it to the school alive. He'd soak them in alcohol, pin them all out—a funeral fit for pharaohs. He dropped the two survivors into new jars and held them to his hammering chest a moment, then hid them beneath his boxes. *I should have never brought them here.* It was what his father had said when his mother had died of fever in Cape Town. He'd resented the words then, but now his heart twisted with understanding. *This is no place for delicate things.*

When the pile was free of his specimens, he grabbed the broom and swept the floor, keeping watch for any more of his friends. His eyes stung. He squeezed them shut against the rising cloud of dust.

He turned to sweep along the line of beds. Bowles' bed had been shifted, rotated so that it faced the wall, the head of it extending out into the center of the room, askew. Grooves in the floorboards tracked where the metal rails had dragged across the floor. Flakes of white enamel outlined where the bed had been. Blood dotted the corner of the sheet. The crystal geode was missing from the bedside table.

Charley quickly swept the rest of the floor, dumping the dust and shards into the bin by the cupboard. He ran the broom to the closet at the end of the hall and spun down the servants' stairs.

In the infirmary, Master Brown and Matron Grace whispered together in the corner. The rows of beds were full of Charley's sleeping housemates, all but one. The bed where Bowles had slept was empty, the pillow stained with blood.

"Matron, Bowles' bed…" Charley said.

Master Brown rushed forward and dropped his hand to Charley's shoulder, steering him back around toward the door. "I'll escort you to the headmaster," he said.

"But sir, where—" Charley stumbled as the master pushed at his shoulder.

"The headmaster's office is at the end of the North Wing on the first floor, past the other masters' offices and quarters." He pinched Charley's shoulder, spinning him around behind the grand staircase.

"No, sir, I mean where is Ethan Bowles?"

"You may address your concerns to the headmaster."

They walked the length of the corridor. To either side, short narrow doors stood closed against the dark hall. At the end, tall wooden double doors covered the wall. Master Brown pulled a ring of keys from his robe. He fumbled through the tangle, selecting a long iron one, and unlocked the door. Gears creaked as they ground against each other, tumbling open. The doors swung freely on giant hinges.

Charley stood in the doorway, staring into the dark office. He could feel the vast expanse of space around him. Master Brown pushed past him and strode into the dark. He lit a lamp on the table, turning the knob so the wick rose, brightening the circle of light in the room. He gestured to a chair in front of the large desk and walked to a door on the right side of the room. He rapped softly on the door and entered, leaving Charley to quake in his bubble of light.

The room smelled of dust and leather, pipe smoke and parchment. Papers covered the top of the massive desk, spilling from piles of brown envelopes. Behind the desk towered a wall of books, a dim rainbow of tarnished leather and canvas spines. Tall wooden file cases sat beneath the windows, their tops cluttered with dried-out inkwells and long-dead potted plants. Coals glowed in a fireplace to his left, which was flanked by two leather chairs.

Charley twisted in his seat. Behind him, the double doors gaped

open to the dark hallway; the wall surrounding the doors reflected bright squares of light from picture glass. Gilt frames sparkled
above the door, surrounding the solemn faces of the earls and the
headmaster. Charley stood and walked to the rows of pictures.

Fifteen portraits, each of sixty or seventy uniformed boys, ten
masters, and a matron. Deep lines crossed the face of the old matron in the first two pictures, her eyes open wide at the camera, her
wild hair pulled tightly back, breaking free in reaching wisps. The
headmaster stood next to her, his hand on her shoulder. Apart from
the appearance of Matron Grace in newer photographs, each portrait looked the same.

Above the cluster of formulaic school photographs, the painted
portraits of Lord Ward and Headmaster Byrne stared out into the
dark room.

Charley turned and scanned the miles of shelves filled with mot-
tled ancient books, wondering if they all belonged to the headmaster, or if the old earl had left them with the building when he died.

The sound of voices grew from behind the side door. Charley ran
to his seat.

The door opened and Master Brown emerged, followed by the
robed but disheveled Headmaster Byrne. His puff of white hair
swept to one side; his face drooped, eyes shadowed with sleep. A
dingy nightgown peeked from beneath the hem of his dark robe,
trailing frayed threads like a spider's spinneret.

Headmaster Byrne sat in the leather armchair across the vast
desk. The leather groaned, straining at its brass tacks. Master Brown
retreated quietly to the shadows beside the double doors and stood
there, hands clasped behind his back, gut thrust forward. *Does he
think he's a soldier?*

Byrne cleared his throat, and Charley spun back to face the headmaster. "I am given to understand, young Mister Winslow, that you
have been the source of a number of disturbances since your arrival.
Is that correct?" In the lamplight, Byrne's mouth seemed unusually
dark, as though the inside was coated in shadow.

Charley shifted in his seat. "I haven't meant to be, sir. I'm afraid
I've had some difficulty settling in."

"That is an understatement, by all accounts. Tell me what happened this evening. Why, Charley, are we all awake at this hour?"

"Sir, I'm not exactly sure what happened. I heard someone in the room, and I heard them move the bed, and then that someone took my specimen jars and smashed them." The heat of his temper rose in his face.

"You did not smash them? You claim no part in all this?"

"No, sir." His fingernails, ragged from cleaning the floor, cut into his palms. "I wouldn't smash them. They were important to me. I don't know who it was in the room." He didn't dare mention the grey man again.

Headmaster Byrne folded his pale hands under his chin, one finger stroking the stubble on his neck. "What age are you, Charley? Eleven? Twelve?"

"Thirteen, sir."

"Thirteen! That's quite old for a first-year student. Did you not receive any education when you were abroad?"

Charley thought of his collection, of his travels and his nanny's songs and stories. "Not in the traditional sense, sir."

"Oh? And in what nontraditional sense were you educated?"

"I learned about the natural history of many countries in Africa, and about their different cultures."

"I see. Well, that's not going to do you much good in England, is it?" Byrne laughed, and Charley saw that his tongue was indeed black, his teeth subtly blue.

"It doesn't seem to be, sir." He whispered to keep from screaming.

Master Brown scoffed behind him.

Charley's palms stung. He felt his face redden. Headmaster Byrne eyed him.

"No matter. If you work hard, you can catch up. And you don't know where this boy Bowles has gone?"

Charley's eyes widened, his anger evaporating in a flood of concern. "No, sir. I brought his nightclothes to him in the infirmary, for Matron Grace. I haven't seen him since."

"Never mind that. How about the fight with Mullins? Skipping meals? An altercation on the grounds?"

Charley dropped his head and shook it. "Mullins killed one of my specimens. I'm sorry I hit him. I missed dinner because I was polishing shoes. Boys on the grounds—I don't know who they were— they threw rocks at me and Bowles. I'm not looking for trouble, sir."

"Looking or not, you've found it." Byrne pulled a large canvas-bound ledger toward him and flipped it open to a blank page. He licked the nib of his pen, coating his tongue in a fresh layer of indigo-black, and began to write. "We are a living organism at this school, Mister Winslow, and you are not behaving as part of the whole. You are at odds with society." He underlined something in his notes. "Do you know why we do not take holidays? Why we do not permit visitors?"

Charley shook his head. *There's no one to come for me, anyway.* "No, sir."

"It's because we are your family now. This institution prides itself on forming the bonds that unite the future of Britain. Lords and captains, Mr. Winslow. The crown and the sword. Do you understand?"

Charley frowned. *There's more to the future than crowns and swords. More to the past. More to the world.* He doubted Byrne had ever left England. "I'm beginning to, sir."

"You will receive extra duties for the next three weeks. Malcolm, your head of house, will assign them as he sees fit. And you'll receive seven lashes, here and now, at my hand. Do you understand?" He placed a thin sheet of blotting paper over the new record and closed the book, peering at Charley from below a lowered brow.

Charley tensed, his legs aching from the last beating. He groaned. "But—"

Headmaster Byrne raised his eyebrows. "That has just made it ten."

* * *

Charley stood at the breakfast table. The boys around him snickered, inviting him to sit. Charley ignored them, squeezing toast past his dry tongue.

Malcolm swung a long leg onto the wood bench, across from Charley. "Did you hear Bowles is gone?" he asked, grabbing a plate piled high with eggs.

"Gone where? Did they send him home?" Mullins asked.

"Nah, they don't know." Malcolm waved a sausage toward the window. "They say he's done a runner."

"Not surprised. There's one every year. Takes longer than this, usually." A nervous laugh rippled down the table. "Maybe Winslow scared him off with his ghost stories."

"Did you really think Master Brown would fall for that?" Sean Mullins sneered. "The ghost did it?"

Charley reminded himself to breathe and choked on toast crumbs. Malcolm turned to him.

"I thought it'd be you this year. But it's not too late yet." Malcolm chewed his sausage, bright eyes challenging.

"Too late for what?" Charley asked. He bit his lips.

"To run home. Like little Bowlesy and a dozen other first-years, in their time," Malcolm said.

Charley thought of the crisp crust that formed on sand dunes overnight, the smell of goat cooking in a brush fire, the vast wheel of stars over the desert. *Home.* "How could Bowles run all the way to London with a head injury? He couldn't even stand."

"London? I'm pretty sure you'd have to have a head injury to run there," Mullins said. The table erupted in laughter. "Maybe he just ran to join the East Wing ghosts!"

"Yeah, how about we have a look for him there?" another boy said. "Get the gardener's shovels and pry off the window boards."

Sean grinned. "Remember the whipping they gave Pip? Thirty lashes and a train ticket home." He turned to Charley. "This one here can take a beating, though. Maybe you should do it, Charley."

Charley sucked on the inside of his lips and clenched his fists, the ache in his legs and backside begging him not to rise to the bait.

"He should sit in the hack spot," Sean said.

Malcolm nodded. "You're right. Charley." He gestured with a sweep of his hand. "Please take your seat over there."

Charley followed Malcolm's long fingertips to an empty seat

toward the end of the table. Boys snickered as he limped around the table and stood at his new place. The wood of the table was gouged and cut through with deep trenches that had been mortared with the filth of a hundred dinners. His plate wouldn't even lie flat across the damaged surface.

"What happened here?" He hadn't wanted to ask. He hadn't wanted to say anything, but his curiosity betrayed him.

"It's the hack spot. It's been hacked, innit?" There was enough laughter to bring a scowl from the masters dining nearby.

Sean leaned toward Charley and whispered forcefully, so that Charley could smell the juice on his breath. "Mad boy sat there the first year of school. Lost his mind. Heard they had to tie him up in the infirmary to keep him from doing to the students what he done to the table." Sean stabbed a link of sausage and held it in front of Charley's face. "He was the first runner—escaped and took off. Never found him. Some think he's the ghost who haunts the place."

Charley slid his fingers through the grooves in the table.

"Are you like the mad boy, Charles? I think the hack seat suits you." Sean bit into the sausage, spraying Charley's face with grease.

The laughter along the table had faded. Charley felt the weight of the boys' stares.

"I think," Malcolm said, "after morning exercise, we'll need our cricket gear cleaned and our coats brushed." He smiled at Charley, then folded a piece of bread in half and chewed the soft center from it, leaving the empty crust on his plate.

Charley nodded and wondered how long it would have taken Bowles to run to London with a head wound.

* * *

Charley tapped his pen against the paper, leaving little ink drops that looked like a cloud of gnats. He drew legs and wings for them, then a spider's web nearby, a hungry spider. The paper slid out from in front of him. He flinched and the welts on his backside throbbed, making him yelp. Every eye in the room turned to him. The hiss of hidden laughter circled him.

Master Crawley examined Charley's paper. "These are interesting figures. Spiders are indeed masters of geometry—which you never will be, Mister Winslow, if you do not pay attention." He slapped the paper back down onto Charley's desk. "You will calculate for me every angle that you have drawn in this fancy web. For every incorrect answer, you will receive one lash."

Charley slowly stood, feeling as though his backside glowed behind him. "Sir, I'm afraid I've already received the maximum allowed lashes this week." The class laughed again.

Master Crawley's sparse eyebrows raised to meet the bottom of his cap. "Is that so? I suppose you'd best get them all correct, then, or we'll have to take our case before the headmaster. I daresay he's overridden that rule before." He returned to the front of the class, and the students' eyes followed him, back to the board and the lesson Charley had been neglecting.

Charley lowered himself carefully back down into his seat. He stifled the whimper that threatened to draw even more attention to his plight. He stared at the matrix of web he'd sketched across his notes. He'd drawn the web as a circle, which made it easy enough to solve. Certainly much easier than navigating Mediterranean star charts.

He left the paper on the master's desk as he followed the file of students out of the room.

"Charles Winslow."

He felt the master's eyes hook his back. He turned and approached the desk.

"This is not the method I teach."

"I'm sorry, sir. My father taught—"

"Mister Winslow, I understand that you come from a background that might lead you to believe my lessons are unnecessary. You'll need to adjust that way of thinking if you intend to succeed here."

"I'm sorry, Master Crawley. I understand. I've been distracted by some personal matters."

"You have my sympathies, but you need to keep your wits about you. There's no room for distraction on the battlefield."

"Battlefield, sir?"

"Life in general. Day to day."

* * *

The puddles of the previous day had soaked into the ground, leaving the peat grass springy and fresh. Boys crowded the lawns, a handful of cricket matches in play.

Charley wandered. He watched the grass as he walked toward the line of trees in the apple orchard. The leaves were fading, taking on a gold luster. He stopped beneath a tree and peeled back a chip of bark, looking into the rumpled scar where a low branch had long ago been cut. Ants scurried through the folds of wood, racing to the wrinkled apples still hanging in the golden leaves. Their tiny black bodies shone like beads, so small, not like the red giants he'd had in his jar.

"Tha'll find no stones in there." The gardener dropped from the tree, a cluster of dead twigs strapped to his side, a curved blade in his hand.

Charley fell back onto the grass, yelping when his tender bottom hit the ground.

The gardener grinned. "Sorry," he said, reaching to pull Charley to his feet. "What is your quest today, Sir Charley? Has tha come t' collect more stones for your friend?"

"No," Charley said. "My friend, he's…they say he's done a runner."

The gardener's eyebrows drew in to his hooked nose. "That so?"

"Yes. I don't know that I'll be needing those stones after all. But thank you."

The gardener nodded, picking dirt from his nails with the blade. "What fascination does th' tree hold for thee, then? You seemed quite keen on it."

"Oh," Charley said, "insects. I collect them, study them. Like my friend with his rocks. Only…less popular with the matron."

The gardener laughed, tossing his head back. Charley saw a tattered line of puckered, pale skin peek from underneath the kerchief tied round his neck.

Charley felt his own stiff face melt into a smile, his lips splitting.

"I shoveled aside a dozen beasties, at least, lookin' for rocks. Here

I thought th' rocks were in the way of my garden, then th' beasts in the way of the rocks, and now I'll watch for the beasts. Here." The gardener walked off toward an old shed tucked away inside the line of trees. He went inside and pulled out a shovel. It was small, rusty, with a splintered wood handle. He handed it to Charley. "Let's go turn over some o' that dirt. Bound to be creatures creepin' toward the surface, now things are dryin' up."

They walked to the new garden. The gardener picked up his own spade by the side of the patch and they began to dig, stirring the dirt and tossing it.

There were worms aplenty, and ants, spiders, fat white grubs. The gardener rattled off the local names—lace webs and false widows, red ants and earwigs. Charley shared the scientific ones. *Amaurobius fenestralis, Steatoda nobilis. Myrmica rubra, Forficula auricularia.*

"Sounds more like a prayer than a spider," Sam said.

They dug deeper, tossing aside large rocks and stringy lengths of roots.

Something white caught Charley's eye. Thinking it might be another large grub, he spooned it out of the pit and dumped it on the ground. Clumps of dirt fell away.

It was a hand. Small, speckled bone covered in papery skin, bands of dry sinew holding it intact. Charley gasped. He dropped his shovel in the dirt.

The gardener bent over it. He picked it up and held it in front of his face, turning it over.

Charley rocked from foot to foot. "Is that—"

The gardener nodded. "*Manus hominum*," he said, winking. "Aye, it's a hand. I'm sorry. I should've warned you. You know th' school was a church, an abbey afore it belonged to the earls? There are graves all over. Some a dozen-hundred years old, markers long gone. I'll like as not need t' rebury this. Best take it to th' headmaster first." He pulled the kerchief from his neck and wrapped it around the small hand.

"So all these lawns were a graveyard?"

"Oh yeah, 'course. This was th' biggest church for leagues. Most everyone important 'round here was buried at this abbey."

"What did the earls do when they started to live here?" Charley felt very conscious of the ground pressing at the bottom of his feet.

"Piled up the stones under the chapel, in the catacombs. The dining hall, now. Rows and rows of 'em down there."

"They just moved the stones? Not the graves?"

"Nah, can't move the graves. Where would they put 'em? Don't let it worry you. Nowt t' be flayed from a four-hundred-year-old royal horse groom." Sam smiled down at Charley.

"The boys say the abbey is haunted." Charley's eyes flicked to the rows of boarded windows along the East Wing and back to the cloth-wrapped bones in Sam's hand.

"It right fits the recipe for it, but I canna see how it's true."

"Why not?"

"Because I've been here for years and not seen owt mis'sen, and that just isn't fair."

Charley smiled, but the smile withered. "Yeah, but you don't have to sleep there."

"That's true. Never have spent the night inside the big place."

"Not at all?"

"No, sir. The old groundskeeper did, slept in th' attic with th' other servants. But when th' headmaster brought me on, he set me up in an old carriage house straight away. Said it was more practical. I suspect he didn't want me mixing with the students, or even the staff, maybe, on account of—" He patted the dark skin of his cheek. "I was still a lad mis'sen, then. But I didn't argue. Much prefer to have me own space."

"Wish I could have my own space. The dorms are awful."

"I can only imagine. I think I'd rather take me chances wi' the ghosts under the chapel than you horrible students."

Charley laughed. The knot in his chest felt lighter, like it was coming untied. He breathed deep, tasted the orchard air on his tongue, and thought that there might be enough here worth liking that he could call it home—at least for a while.

The chime of the brass bell rolled across the grounds.

"Could you…"

"Yes?" Sam looked up. He'd begun to fill in the hole where

Charley had removed the hand.

Charley saw the skin of his neck, red and puckered in a thick line across his throat. Charley stared.

"What does tha need?" Sam asked.

Charley tore his eyes from the gardener's throat, looked into his dark eyes. "Might you not mention I was with you, when you found it? I'm supposed to be blending in, and I'm not doing very well." Charley dropped his gaze to his boots, to the mud caked in the laces, anything to avoid looking at the hand wrapped in the kerchief, at the gardener's scarred neck.

"Aye, I understand. Not a problem."

"And…you might lock up your tools. When you're not digging, I mean. Some of the boys mentioned them—said they'd seen them around and could take them."

Sam frowned, but nodded. "Best run along, lest th' headmaster sees you, or one of his spies does. Off you go," Sam said, climbing to his feet. "Back to your horrible peers and haunted halls. I'll go back to me turnips."

Charley hurried back toward the school. As he walked across the flagstones, he thought of the hundreds of graves under his feet. He tried to step as quietly as possible. *I wouldn't like it if my stone was moved.*

He ran inside and up to his dorm, and sat on his bed, heart racing, panting, coughing from the cold damp in his lungs. Boys would soon file into the building, head to their studies to read and review or smoke and talk.

Charley stood. He walked along the rows of beds, reaching under and pulling out pairs of shoes. Under Bowles' bed, there were two pairs. He pulled them out. One set still shone from the last time Charley had polished them. The other was caked in mud, spattered with rain water and blood.

Bright red ants swarmed the blood spots. The electric lights blazed off their fiery backs.

Charley dropped his load of shoes and knelt on the floor, peering under the bed. A trail of ants marched beneath, from the drops of blood to the wall, and along the baseboard around the perimeter of the room. Charley followed them.

They led out into the hall, a few yards down, and into the broom closet. He pulled at the knob and the door swung open. The row of ants marched to the back of the closet and through a small gap in the back corner of the wall.

Charley pressed his hands against the wall, leaning in toward his determined friends. The wall shifted. The boards were cool to the touch. He felt around the edges, slipping his finger into the hole at the corner. The plank of wood lifted. He pulled, and the wide board fell away.

Behind it lay a dark, drafty platform and a plummeting tunnel. Ants swarmed, black and red alike, over the space behind the wall. In the dim light from the hall, Charley saw a dark pool on the tunnel floor. It smelled foul. He knelt and blew gently on the crowd of ants. They scrambled back, scattering away.

He reached out. The puddle was dark and sticky. He pulled his finger from its tacky surface and brought it to his nose.

Blood.

CHAPTER THREE

Charley backed away from the swarming platform. He pushed the plank back in place, kicking it closed, then ran back to the dormitory.

He grabbed Bowles' bed and pulled it from the wall. Droplets of dried blood had been spattered across the floor beneath it, blending into the wood grain. Charley leaned over the stains. Whoever had moved the bed must have dripped the blood as they did it. He crouched, studying the pattern. *Ghosts don't bleed.*

Malcolm walked into the room. "What are you doing, Charley?"

"I was getting shoes to polish. I forgot and went to get Bowles' shoes, and—look." Charley held up his hand, blood smeared across his fingertips.

Malcolm walked over and leaned down, his long hair cloaking his face. He took Charley's hand, sniffed at his finger, and bent over the spots on the floor. "Probably just from his head injury. Or from your arm. I heard about what happened. Crey was bragging at dinner. I'm sorry I thought…Thanks for helping Bowles get to the infirmary."

Charley nodded, unsure what to say. "If this was from his head, though, how did it get under the bed? It must have dripped here when the bed was moved."

"Maybe he moved his bed to get his things before he ran off?"

"He didn't take his things. Look, his tack box, with all his rocks."

"Yeah, well, if I was running off, I'd leave a box of rocks behind, too."

"Well, you're not Ethan Bowles. He loves those rocks. I don't think it was him that moved this. He wasn't well. Besides—how's he meant to have run to London with no shoes?" Charley looked at the blood on his finger. His hand shook as he thought about the space behind the wall. He didn't want to tell Malcolm. *He's kind now, but in front of the others…* The echo of a lashing rippled across the backs of his thighs.

"What exactly are you saying, Charley?"

"I'm not sure, really. Have you heard the person who comes in here at night? Have you seen him? The grey figure—the one who keeps breaking things. I don't believe he's a ghost."

Malcolm's eyes narrowed, searching Charley's face. "What class are you missing right now?"

Charley flinched. "Latin, I think."

Malcolm walked to the bookshelf. He pulled down the first-year book of Latin text. "I'll say you're ill. Copy the entire glossary, for missing class. And get some rest."

Charley took the text, smearing blood across the cover.

* * *

Sam cradled the delicate curl of bone in his palm as he walked down the long masters' hall toward the double doors. He feared that if he walked too quickly it would lift and blow from his hand, shatter on the thin carpet. He stared at the papery skin, tied to the small bones with leathery ligament cords. The others had been dustier. More bone, less leather.

He paused in front of the headmaster's doors. He raised the small hand to his nose and sniffed. Earth and stone—but still something else…

The lever on the door rattled, and the carved panel swung open.

Sam quickly placed his other cupped hand over the bones. *No need for anyone else to see this.*

Headmaster Byrne appeared at the door. "Sam. What are you doing here?"

"I'm sorry t' bother you, Headmaster. I was working on the new vegetable patch and I found this, buried in the dirt." He lifted his hand off the bit of skeleton.

The headmaster's lips thinned. "Another? Well, what of it? I take it you have the proper tools to rebury it."

"Yes, sir, but this one—it's a bit different than th' others."

"What do you mean?"

"It isn't as old. Smell."

"I most certainly will not! Take that thing away."

Sam looked at the hand, then traced the lines in the headmaster's face. He had been kind, once, when Sam was a boy.

"Sorry, Sam. You just surprised me, that's all." He sighed. "It was probably just in a boggy patch of the old abbey cemetery. Better preserved. Now take it to your little burial plot and give it a prayer." Byrne's tense face twisted into an ugly smile.

"O' course, sir. I'll have the chaplain—"

"No, he's busy. We're off to lecture some boys right now. Do it yourself, Sam, and keep it between us. We don't need the students getting scared—or, worse, deciding to look for more."

Sam nodded. He wrapped the little fist back up in his handkerchief and covered the parcel with his hands.

Byrne stepped past Sam, pulled the heavy door closed, and locked it. Sam watched his robes float behind him as he strode off down the hall.

There was a muffled laugh behind the locked door.

Sam jumped and stumbled away from it. His heart hammered. He felt movement in his hands, and realized he'd squeezed his fingers shut in fear. Small pieces of bone shifted beneath the handkerchief. *Oh no. No no no.*

That smell—the one hiding beneath the scent of earth—intensified. It wasn't bog. Sam knew bog.

* * *

Behind the pile of discarded rocks, beyond the long arm of the East Wing, stood a ring of ash and thorn trees. Sam stood in its center, digging a small hole. All around him were shards of shale sticking out of the ground in neat rows, a crooked cross scratched into each.

A cold mist had consolidated into rain. Sam shook the water from his eyes and used the shovel to spoon the growing puddle from the deepening hole. His gaze wandered to the crumpled handkerchief and its broken contents.

Wonder if your arm is here. Or your leg or your teeth, in my little bone field.

He'd buried every stray bone here. *A different sort of garden altogether.*

"Old priests," the headmaster had said, "or their servants. Local lords. An abbey must have a graveyard."

When the hole was deep enough, Sam lowered the little fist into the earth and covered it over. He stood and stared through the rain at the crumbled and boarded-over façade of the East Wing. He whispered a quiet prayer. It sounded more like spiders than prayers.

* * *

Sam stood outside the infirmary door. His breath fogged in the cold air evaporating from his wet clothes. He dripped muddy rainwater over the threshold. He knocked.

Matron Grace's blue eye appeared around the edge of the door.

"Sam, what are you doing here?"

Why do they all ask me that? This is me home.

"Sorry to bother you, Grace. I wonder if you might have a spare strip o' cloth, a bandage, maybe."

"Are you hurt?" More of her face appeared as she stepped closer, pulled the door open wider.

Sam paused. He rubbed at the wet cloth of his upturned collar. *No need for anyone else to see this, neither.* "Yes—a bit, I guess. Nothing bad, mind. I just...need a bit o' cloth."

Matron Grace nodded once. "Just a moment, please." The door closed. The click of her heels receded from the threshold, then returned. Her pale hand slipped through the small opening, a roughspun bandage pinched in her delicate fingers.

Sam gasped. He saw the fingers curled, as bone. He rubbed his muddy fists across his eyes.

"Sam?" Grace had opened the door wider, her face creased with concern. "Do you need me to examine you?"

He blinked at her. She was flesh again. "Thank you," he said, and plucked the bandage from her fingers. He spun and trudged down the hall, leaving wet boot prints across the thin, faded carpet. He could feel her cold eyes boring into his back, felt the cold marble eyes of the earls slide over him.

He slipped around a corner, out of sight. The damp wool of his collar poured fresh water down his neck as he folded the fabric back. He shivered.

Fingers trembling, he tied the strip of bandage around his neck, over his scar.

* * *

The long column of boys, led and followed by cars full of robed masters, marched down the stony lane away from the school, toward the village where the headmaster would dedicate the new chapel funded and built by the Old Cross School. "Newhaven" was its name, and it was meant to replace the Old Cross Chapel as the local place of worship. The people born and raised in the village had lost their church when the earl had left it to the school. The replacement had been a long time coming.

Mud is even harder to march in than sand. Dunes don't steal your boots or wet your socks.

The rain had stopped and the mist had mostly cleared, except for low under the trees. Charley watched its shifting shapes under the orchard rows as he marched. Worms floated to the top of the mud; he fought to resist the urge to bend and scoop them up. They wouldn't last long in his pockets, and he'd be spotted for certain.

Masters Brown and Crawley walked along the marching stream of students, barking at anyone who fell out of step. Master Culvert brought up the rear, falling further behind as they marched.

"This isn't a country stroll; it's an exercise," they'd been warned.

The village was three miles away, across the expansive abbey park and surrounding moor. A remnant of ancient forest beyond that masked the small gathering of rooftops from view, though their smoke was visible from the third floor on cold days. Sean claimed to read smoke signals from the village girls—love notes broadcast to the sky. He'd pretend to read them aloud, to the horror of its intended recipient. He'd never chosen Charley. "No one knows who you are," he'd said.

I prefer it that way. But then Charley thought of Ethan Bowles, and his heart sank. *People know me. Then they leave.*

"In step, Winslow!"

Charley shook free of his thoughts. The village was visible now, the bell tower of the new chapel taller than anything else on the horizon.

They gathered on a crescent of lawn and gravel in front of the tall stone edifice, its mortar still clean, walls untouched by vine or moss. *How long has it been since Old Cross looked like this?*

There were chairs assembled, but they were saved for the village elderly—those who had been, as babes, baptized where Charley now ate his toast. They stared up at the new chapel, heads trembling on thin shoulders.

One woman had spun in her seat and stared back at the rows of boys, scanning their faces. One of her eyes was clouded, the other clear and piercing, now boring into the headmaster as he made his way through the crowd to the front, where a shiny new lectern had been dragged from inside. A bright ribbon crossed the banded wood doors to the chapel.

The headmaster cleared his throat and waited for the crowd to settle.

The milk-eyed woman had turned forward again. Charley studied the back of her head. Her hair had been yellow once, like his mother's, though she was far older than his mother would have been. Even her shoulders carried the disapproval he'd seen in her face.

He supposed not every village resident was fond of the new church. No doubt many still wished to worship at the abbey, as their ancestors had done. Charley reeled at the thought. The longest he had ever called one place home had been the house in Cape Town, where he and his mother had tended the same patch of garden for three springs in a row, long enough to know what each plant was when it was only just sprouted. He remembered the moment when he realized he knew where each garden flagstone was—that he could find his way in the dark. He tried to think of what it must be like to always know, to always have known. To have lived your whole life in the same footsteps, the ones your father and grandfather and his father had walked. It was, all at once, overwhelming. Charley's footsteps had covered more land than eight generations of these farmers had tilled.

The sudden silence of the crowd shook Charley from his thoughts. The crowd met the stern gaze of the headmaster. *He looks at his elders the same way he looks at his students.* Charley trained his ears toward the copse of trees planted in the lawn, ringed with dying flowers. Even in the chill, he heard the hum of industry, the buzz of autumn insects. He hadn't been able to smuggle a jar from the breakfast table.

The headmaster began to holler about new beginnings, about gifting new generations with new traditions. The villagers clapped softly, but not enough to drown out the hum of flies.

Headmaster Byrne turned and cut the bright ribbon. The elders stood and shuffled up the steps, leaning on the arms of attending students.

All but the milk-eyed woman. She stood, shaking, staring at a side-yard opposite the trees where a wide expanse of lawn stretched, ready to accept the village dead.

Charley approached her and held out his arm. She stared into his face. He saw his own sense of gravity mirrored there. He nodded, and she took his arm.

"Do you know him?" Charley asked, nodding to the headmaster, who stood on the stairs greeting each villager who entered the church.

"Nearly married him," she croaked.

Charley paused and had to recover his pace. "Nearly? What happened?"

"We'll say a younger, richer lass was 'faster' than I."

"I didn't know he had a wife."

"He didn't. She wasn't the marrying type. Neither was he, apparently."

"If you'll pardon me," Charley led her to the foot of the stairs, where she balked. "I think you dodged a bullet there."

She laughed then, a broken sound, and patted Charley's hand. The fingers of her right hand were all missing their final joint. She ran her shortened hand over the stone wall beside her. "Whoever sits in the big chair at the fancy house owns the village. It's more than tradition—it's habit. Be careful what you say around here, lad. The walls have ears, and Byrne owns all the tongues."

The headmaster was now surrounded by the village police, shaking hands and laughing.

"Where did you meet him?" Charley asked.

"I worked for the earl at the big house. Byrne was his friend. He lived here in the village with his brother, a doctor. When his brother left for London, he took over their family house, though he spent more time at the abbey."

"And the villagers don't like that it's a school?"

"I daresay he's won most of them over now. We village folk may have long memories, but we're right good at forgetting the past when it suits us. He's a local boy. He's built them a new church. He's taken on the upkeep of the abbey."

"Except for the East Wing."

She shot Charley a sidelong glance.

"Did you ever see it when you worked there?" Charley kept his eyes on their place in line as they advanced up the stairs toward the headmaster.

"I have. I did. It was already closed off when I started, just barely. The lady of the house had recently died, but you know children. They'd always find a way in, and I'd have to come fetch them out."

"There's a way in?" Charley's heart hammered. They were nearly at the top of the stairs, eyes level with Byrne's scuffed shoes. Soon they'd be in his range of hearing.

"For every way m'lord blocked, they seemed to find two more. Just like little mice, they were."

"They? I thought the earl only had a daughter."

"He had a son too, briefly. And then his daughter, and her—well. Poor man died of grief, if you ask me."

Charley stared at the buttons on the headmaster's waistcoat. He had more questions, a thousand more—more than when they had begun talking, but they were next in line. The woman's grip tightened on his arm, pinching till it hurt.

He shook Byrne's hand. The old woman shook it and stared deep into his face. If Byrne recognized her, he didn't let on. His attention passed to the people behind them, and they were herded into the church.

Masters, students, and villagers milled around them, reciting local histories depicted in the stone and glass. A bust of Byrne, even more elaborately carved than the one in the school entrance hall, sat on a plinth in an alcove. Baskets of hothouse roses sat around it, giving a bitter lift to the sour smell of the crowd.

As they finished their circuit of the large room, the crowd began to fill the long pews. Special seats had been reserved at the back for students. Charley didn't want to leave the old woman.

"May I write to you? I have questions about…local history." Charley walked the woman to a seat at the front of the church.

"Wouldn't dare send my answers in writing to that place. Best you don't mention me. But you know where to find me if you need help." She patted Charley's hand with her shortened fingers again and pulled her arm from his.

The local vicar had taken his position, and stared down his nose at anyone still making their way to a seat. Charley squeezed onto the end of a crowded pew. It still smelled of fresh varnish and felt tacky, as if it hadn't yet cured.

The sermon began. Charley's thoughts wandered to the earl's dead wife, and their son that no one spoke of. His cast-aside daughter.

A swelling ache bloomed in his chest. He wondered what his father was doing now. Crouched behind a wall, gun in hand? Marching patrols through desert dunes? He wondered if his father had time to think of him, or if the distraction of battle required his every thought. Charley didn't want to be a distraction, but he wanted to be thought of.

The crowd rose and sang a song that Charley didn't know. He sang his nurse's lullaby instead, quietly. They filed into the aisle for bread and wine. Charley tried to catch the old woman's eye as he walked past, but her eyes were squeezed shut, her lips moving in rapid prayer.

Afterward, the boys were held last while the villagers dispersed, walking home along paths they'd use for centuries, laying down footsteps their children and their children's children would follow. It might be a new path for them now, but it was home.

As the students marched back toward the school, weary from the fresh air, wind, and mud, Charley counted the drowned worms in the standing water of their morning footprints. A few boys cheered at the sight of the school's tall bell tower. Charley, too, felt relief—a sense of homeness, maybe. It quickly drained, and dread took its place. He used the diversion of the cheering boys to dip down and grab a few worms to slip into his pocket. They were limp, dead, but juicy. His ants would eat well.

* * *

"Oik!" A marble hit Charley, bounced off his shoulder, and rolled into his blankets. "My foot hurts, and I'm thirsty." Sean grinned at him from a pile of pillows, his bandaged foot elevated like a trophy.

Charley climbed off his bed and went to the water pitcher.

"Nah, nah." Another marble snapped off the back of Charley's head. Heat rose in his face. "I don't want water. Go to the kitchens and get me a bottle of whisky."

Charley turned and frowned at Sean. Malcolm hid behind his long hair and toyed with the ratty binding of a magazine.

"I don't think they keep—"

"*They* don't keep it. The headmaster keeps it. Pull up the flagstone right in front of the oven. It's in a cellar down there."

Charley wondered if this was a ploy—a plot to get him caught out of bounds and caned again. A thought occurred to him.

He pictured the stone of the kitchen floor: the same as the dining hall, as the chapel. "Are there gravestones in the cellar, too?" The boys stared at Charley. Malcolm's eyes even appeared over the top of his magazine. He felt his face get warmer.

"Yeah, sure," Sean said. "They keep the corpses right between the booze and the apples." A few boys laughed, but most continued to stare.

"It's just, I heard…never mind." Charley turned away from the prying eyes. *Just because this idiot didn't see them doesn't mean they aren't there.*

* * *

The weight of the flagstone dug into Charley's fingertips. The stone itself smelled like warm bread, but the hollow below it smelled of damp earth.

Charley lowered his feet into the shadows and swung them onto the rung of an angled ladder. His hand shook, and hot wax dripped onto his fingers from the candlestick. As he stepped onto an earthen floor, light flickered off dusty jars and bottles. He gently blew the dust from the labels until he found the amber label of the whisky. He pulled the bottle from the shelf, and his candlelight stretched into the space behind it—into far too much space. The darkness behind the shelves deepened, with no visible end.

Charley dropped to his knees and pushed aside rows of jars. The cellar continued far beyond the shelves. He reached into the empty space and pulled himself through. His stomach dragged against the grit on the neglected shelf, stirring a cloud of dust that threatened to choke him.

Beyond the planks, his fingers ploughed through loosely-packed soil. The candle guttered but stayed lit, casting dancing shadows deep into the empty space. Charley climbed to his feet. The smell of earth and dust was richer here, away from the cellar wares.

He cast the light around and made his way to a wall of stacked, crumbling stone. Along the wall, at intervals, were long, dusty alcoves. Splintered shards of wood were scattered inside the empty spaces. Charley peered into each, walking back farther and farther into the dark room.

He could see the leaning stack of stones long before he reached them. They lay in layers against the far wall, each row at least fifty deep. *I'm under the chapel. This is the catacombs. These are the missing stones.*

He brushed his fingers across the face of a stone in front of him. Dust and web and crumbling stone came away at his fingertips. He traced an inscription, no longer visible. *You're out there, somewhere. Under the stomping feet of boys. Are you looking for your stone?* He brushed more dust from the top.

"Rachel, damn you, girl. Are you down there?"

Charley's knees buckled, and he dropped to the dusty floor. Wood splinters drove into his knees.

Bright lantern light crept down the ladder. Charley blew out his candle and crouched in the darkness.

The wide shadow of the cook prowled the space beyond the shelves. Charley spotted her red kerchief bobbing past the shelves. Malcolm had said it used to be regulation white, but she used it to wipe butchering blood from her hands. "Rachel, that you down here?"

Charley held his breath. He prayed she wouldn't notice the messed shelves, or the trail in the dust where he'd slipped between the glass jars.

Her gravelly voice grew quiet and rhythmic. She was counting.

"Goddamn little monsters!" she growled. The light rose back up the ladder and disappeared. The flagstone scraped back into place.

Charley was plunged into darkness. His heart raced. He gripped the cooling candle in his fist and inched his way through the dirt toward the barrier of shelves. His fingers scraped along the floor. They slipped into a pile of loose pebbles that dug into his palm, sticking like barbs. He paused to catch his breath and still his pounding pulse, turning the pebbles over in his hand. They were smooth-surfaced, long, pointed. Charley began to feel faint. He ran his fingers over the small stones. Teeth. He was sure that they were teeth.

He pushed himself to his feet and ran, his clenched fists ahead of him until he collided with the rack of shelves. Glass jars rang against each other, rocked, and thudded into the dirt as he pushed his way through the rows of preserves. He felt his way to the ladder and scrambled up, heaving the flagstone away with his shoulders.

The cook was gone. A cracked basket sat on the table, overflowing with dry, discarded bread crusts and chicken bones. The scent of rot overpowered the warm bread smell from the hearth. Dim light from the hall stretched into the kitchen, and he followed it, heart and feet never slowing until he burst into the dormitory.

Sean and Malcolm turned to him. The rest of the boys slept, or feigned it.

He realized he'd forgotten the whisky, abandoned it in the dirt of the crypt. He looked down at his hands. He was filthy, covered in dirt and dust. In his fist, he clutched a handful of ancient teeth.

A shoe struck his face. The teeth flew from his fist and scattered across the ring of marbles at his feet.

"We lied for you. Told the master you were in the loo." Malcolm handed him a cool cloth. Sean turned away and pulled his blanket over his shoulder.

"He was looking for me?"

"He was checking the dorms. Said there was a student in the kitchens. How'd you escape?"

Charley still wasn't certain he was meant to have escaped. "I hid in the crypt."

Malcolm's eyes darted to Charley, then resumed their downward cast. "The hell you did."

"I did!"

"Quiet!"

They listened for movement in the dark hall. Nothing stirred.

"It's behind the pantry shelves," Charley said. "There aren't any bodies anymore. Not really. Just the stones they removed from the yard."

Malcolm shook his head. "Thought I'd been everywhere in this school."

"Have you?" Charley raised his eyebrows, felt the sore spot where the shoe had struck him.

"Guess not, have I? You've barely been here a month and you go and find a whole room I've never seen."

Charley wanted to ask him if he knew about the tunnel behind the broom cupboard down the hall, but not now. "Have you been inside the East Wing?"

"Course I have."

A thousand questions tangled in Charley's mouth.

"No one respects a head boy who hasn't seen inside the East Wing."

Charley's mind finally settled on a question. "What did you see?"

"It's just a broken old building, Charley. Just rubbish."

"How did you get in?" His whisper caught, half-formed. He'd been holding his breath without noticing.

Malcolm's head jerked to the end of the hall. At first Charley thought it was an answer, but then he saw the glow of light rising in the servants' staircase. The master's lantern.

Malcolm punched out the light and made for his bed, but Charley grabbed his arm. "How did you get in?"

Charley couldn't see Malcolm's face in the dark room, but he could feel him weigh the question. Around them, sleeping boys sighed.

"You gotta climb. Up, and through a window. The nailed boards are loose, and some have fallen clear off. Most of the windows don't have glass anymore."

Charley released his arm.

"But there's nothing to see, Charley. It's a ruin."

* * *

Sam handed Charley an apple. "Won't be many more fresh this year, so enjoy it," he said.

"I haven't been in England for winter since I was four," Charley said. "I don't remember it, really." He settled himself against the stone wall, his head well below the top, as his father had taught him to hide in foxholes. Sam crouched beside him, all but the top of his hat sheltered from the view of the school.

"You'll freeze. 'Nesh' we call it, moaning about the cold. I've spent a good number o' my winters right here at this school."

"Were you a student here?"

Sam laughed. "No. Never been a student anywhere. I was a wanderin' tramp all across Yorkshire. Settled here when I was sixteen. Headmaster felt sorry for me and took me on as staff. Been here ten years now. It's home."

Charley looked over the expanse of grounds: fields and forest, hills and moors. He could see how it could become a home, in time. "Where did you wander from? And why all the way out here?"

Sam let loose a deep breath. He took a bite of apple, leaving a smudge of dirt against the fruit. "I came here looking for me mam. I'd heard she'd come here t' the school, thought maybe I'd find her." He twisted the stem of his apple, pulled it free.

"You didn't find her?"

"No. By the time I got here, she'd moved on. She'd been the matron here for two terms, then she was dismissed. Headmaster wouldn't say why, though I've heard things. No one's heard nowt from her since. Some folks in town say she talked of going to London." Sam shrugged. "I decided not to follow. Not anymore. Felt I should be here. Like I belonged, in a way. There's summat about the place."

Charley plucked the pips from his apple core. "Why were you separated? Why had she come here without you?"

"It's a long story. Not a nice one."

"I have a bad story. It's not long, but I'll trade you." Charley rolled a pip between his fingers and dropped it in his pocket.

Sam smiled. He rubbed his hands over his face and pulled at his beard. "Me dad was a captain, like yours. He fought in the siege at Khartoum. He was part of the local base—earned himself some honors and a house in England. Not a big house, but land. He'd left me mam pregnant with me when he went back to war. I was all of five years old when he come back, wounded. My mother cared for him, and for me, and then she had twins. Two boys, both with dark curls." He smiled for a moment, then sighed. "I think that wore her out, in the end. She wasn't used to working so hard. She'd come from an old, wealthy family and had been disowned for runnin' off with my father and having a baby out o' wedlock—because of me, I suppose. One day she wouldn't get out of bed. My father shouted at her, called her unkind things. He was in pain all the time and lost his temper right quick. She got up then and took a knife, and she cut his throat. Then the two babes. Then me. They all died, but I didn't. I don't remember much. I guess a neighbor come by and took me to hospital, where they stitched me up." Sam pulled a strip of linen aside, and Charley saw the thick scar more closely, slashed across his neck. The skin bunched and rippled, with dirt gathered in the creases.

Charley shuddered, his apple poised, forgotten in front of his face.

"I grew up working for the neighbor that found me, doing chores, apprenticed to her husband, a glass worker. When I was sixteen, I decided to try and find me mam. The police had looked for her. I followed their trail and found more on my own. This is where I lost her."

Charley set his apple on his knee. "I'm sorry." His throat tightened around the bite of apple he tried to swallow. "And I'm afraid my story is a poor trade for yours."

"Well, let's hear it. You can owe me the balance later." The sun had dipped behind the school, turning their space behind the fence into a tent of shadow.

Charley's heart fluttered, and he wondered, suddenly, if he should tell. *I could tell him about my mother instead.* But his worry for Bowles won out.

"I found blood upstairs. Quite a lot of it, behind a loose board at the back of a closet."

Sam's face hardened. "Did you tell anyone?"

"Not about the closet. I found more blood under Bowles' bed. His bed had been moved, turned around last night, about the time he went missing. I was reaching under to get his shoes to polish, and there was blood there on the edge, and when I moved the bed, I saw it was everywhere. I showed Malcolm, the head boy. He says it was probably just from his head wound, but there was too much of it there, behind that wall."

Sam took a knife from his pocket and carved slices from another apple. The crease at his brow grew deeper as the silence stretched. He handed some to Charley. "I took that hand to th' headmaster. He told me to rebury it, say a prayer for the soul I'd disturbed. Thing is, it came apart a bit in my scarf, and I don't think it's as old as I thought. A few years, maybe. But too much of it left for the old abbey days."

Charley took an apple slice and chewed it slowly. "What did the headmaster say to that?"

"He's not a man t' be questioned." Sam peeled at the skin of the apple, drawing it away from the meat.

"Malcolm says a boy runs away every year. Says they run home."

"That I can believe. Did Bowles have family near here?"

"His gran's in London. His dad is in Cairo with mine."

"Maybe your dad knows his. Maybe his dad will have heard if he's back in London."

Charley sat up, shifting his position on the crumbling pile of stones. "We're meant to write home tomorrow. I'll ask my dad if he knows a Bowles at base."

"If he doesn't, we can find out who his gran is, write t' her and see if he's there."

"How do we find out where she is? There's bound to be a hundred Bowles in London."

The gardener's eyes twinkled, though his face was lined and grim. "Th' headmaster'd know."

"He won't tell me," Charley said. The rock wall dug into his fading bruises.

"No, he won't. But he'll have writ it down somewhere." Sam smiled.

Charley smiled back, handing Sam a small handful of apple seeds. "But what about the hole in the wall? The tunnel? Where does it go, do you think?"

"This is an old place. Bound t' be full of holes and tunnels. Hidden walkways for staff, servants—hidey-holes for the old priests. Best not t' go in there, Charley. I doubt they're maintained. Likely not safe."

"But the blood..."

"Maybe a cat caught a mouse there, or even dragged a bird in," Sam said

"But if Bowles went that way—"

"I doubt he did, Charley. Likely only the housemaids even know it's there. See to your letter. Home is probably where you'll find your friend."

* * *

Charley sketched the spokes of a chariot wheel, so like a spider's web, as Master Crawley gestured, wildly expressing a tale of Apollo reclaiming his chariot and raising the sun. His copy of Ovid's *Metamorphoses* lay open in front of him, with one page in English facing a page in Latin. A portrait of Apollo stared out at him from the bottom of the Latin text: empty-eyed, straight-nosed, laurel-wreathed, and radiating beams of light.

"And what do you find significant in this tale, Winslow?" Master Crawley stared intently at him.

"Sir?"

"The stories have a purpose. A lesson. What has this story taught you?"

Charley thumbed the fill-lever on his pen, dropping a bead of ink on his paper. "That these gods were reckless with their world. They threatened all existence for petty arguments." The class stifled laughter.

"The lesson, Charles Winslow, is about obedience to the gods. It's about the natural order of things and the punishment of those who subvert it."

"Oh. Sorry, sir. That's just not how I heard the story."

"Really? Please, enlighten us with your obscure translation of divine legend."

Charley imagined his father's breath against his ear, hot and scented with goat's meat, as he whispered translations of their hosts' tales, narrating stories that dancers performed. He remembered the smoke in his eyes and the grit of dirt in his teeth as he smiled. His heart beat the drum rhythm of the fireside dance.

He realized he was smiling. The class awaited his answer. "In the story I heard, the sun dropped down to the earth because he loved her. And it was the children who lifted him back up into the sky."

The professor rubbed at his chin, smearing it with chalk dust. "I've never heard such a tale. Where did you read this?"

"I didn't read it, sir. I watched it—heard it."

"A play?"

"Of sorts, sir."

"Well then, by all means, perform a bit for us. Performance is a mythic tradition."

Charley's face slicked with cold sweat. He stood from his bench. He stomped his feet—the hollow, dusty planks of the risers a poor substitute for the beat against sand. He slammed his hand down on the desk and began to sing as his nurse had taught him. The class erupted in laughter. Charley's face reddened and he dropped back into his chair, his song unfinished.

"That was not Latin or Greek, Winslow." The professor's brow lowered at him. "I highly doubt you saw this performed in London."

"In London? No, sir. It isn't Greek; it's Saan. In Khoisan. From South Africa."

The professor dropped his hands and coughed, sending a cloud of chalk dust down his waistcoat. "Then it's hardly relevant to this course of study, is it? You've wasted all our time with this diversion. Remain after class and copy the text from Ovid. You *will* correct your learning. It is my duty to see it done." He turned to resume the lesson.

Charley flipped through his text to see how long the passage stretched. It was a long one. "Here Phaethon lies who in the sun-god's chariot fared. And though greatly he failed, more greatly he dared…"

These gods cherish foolishness. Anansi would have sucked them dry.

As if in answer, a spider dropped from a ceiling beam and dangled over the professor's head, just as he drew Zeus's bolt piercing Phaeton's heart.

* * *

Charley's letter went unanswered. He passed the weeks filching jelly jars from the breakfast table and filling them with the last few insects of autumn, hiding them under Bowles' bed, which had become a repository for the other boys' cast-off clothes and soiled cricket gear. The missing boy had been forgotten by all but Charley, and the other boys had settled into a natural pace, revolving like an indifferent vortex around the empty bed. Only Charley seemed to feel the weight of the emptiness.

Charley hid in the orchards, wrapped warmly against the encroaching cold, while the boys raced across the open grounds or marched in small regiments, practicing the drills they hoped to perform one day in imitation of their fathers.

"I should have heard by now," he said, tying knots in the tassels of his scarf.

Sam stood above him on a ladder, pruning the tree. "May take a while, if there's any action goin' on. May not be any mail comin' or goin'." He tied down a small branch, training it to twist toward a thin space in the foliage.

"What if Bowles is hurt? I think we should find his gran. I think we should have done that in the beginning. I don't think I can wait anymore."

"Fair enow. We can do that. But we'll have to break some rules."

"How do we do it?"

Sam dropped a small branch at Charley's feet. Charley picked it up and set it on the pile in the wheelbarrow.

"If I get you a key to th' headmaster's office, could you sneak in there and look up Bowles' file? You'll have to memorize th' address. Put it right back in place. He's a particular man. Might spot a change." Sam climbed down the ladder, brushing leaves from his hair.

"Yes, I think I could do that. If there's a diversion, too—something amiss at the time—I could pretend to be there to report it, if I'm caught."

Sam nodded. "That should work. I'll flood the lawn below your window. You can say you noticed it and feared damage to the grounds and walls."

"Perfect. Can we do it tonight?" Charley looked up at him, at the pieces of leaf still caught in his black curls.

Sam scratched his beard. "Aye, I can get the key for tonight, if you want. I watch the grounds when all the masters are away on holidays, so I have access to the staff storage. There's a spare set of keys there. I don't think they're used often."

"Leave the key in the entrance hall, behind the bust of Byrne." Charley wrung his hands. The full measure of the risk he was about to take was beginning to dawn on him.

"I will. And I'll go set up me pump. When you see the lawn flooded, head out. It'll take a while, but we'll need to be sure all the off-duty masters are asleep."

Charley nodded. He followed Sam across the lawn, watching the groove where the wheelbarrow cut through the grass.

Sam stopped. "Charley, I can't promise that they won't cane you if you're caught. If you see someone, hide. We can always try another plan, another night."

Charley smiled wryly and looked him in the eye. "My last caning was ten strikes."

Sam flinched.

"On the one hand, I'll be sure to avoid it if possible. On the other, I know I can handle it."

Sam smiled and saluted. Charley returned the salute.

* * *

Charley sat on his bed. He gently stretched the legs of a dead garden spider, setting them in place, pinning them to rough canvas. In the flicker of candlelight, the spider seemed to dance, tapping out a story rhythm of the afterlife.

He listened to the breathing of his sleeping roommates, now familiar, the song of every night. He hummed.

A soft splashing sounded outside, below his window.

The tap-tap-tap and wavering light of the master on duty drew near. Charley blew out the candle and lay down, breathing slowly, rising after the light had passed.

He walked to the window. Moonlight shone across a field dotted with mirrors of standing water.

He grabbed a pile of clothes from Bowles' bed and stuffed them under his blanket, arranging them like his sleeping form. He pulled on his sweater, stepped into his slippers, and leaned against the wall inside the door to the hallway.

Peeking out of the room, he could see the master's light shining off the wood varnish far down the hall. The light vanished around the curve of the grand staircase.

Charley stepped out into the shadows and edged down the hall, away from the light, toward the back of the wing and the curving servants' stairs. He felt his way through the dark, running his hand along the wall, feeling the edge of each step with his toes.

When he reached the ground floor, he sneaked through the quiet kitchens. The coals in the ovens still glowed warm, the smell of bread and onion soaked into the brick walls.

He crept down the back hallway till he felt the soft rolled edge of carpet under his feet. He followed it, back against the long wall, until he felt the space around him open into the tall entryway, the quality of air turning vast and hollow.

A faint glow from the main staircase suffused the dim entryway with a dull light. Charley slid along the perimeter of the room to the long row of columns supporting busts of the earls, who'd lived in the old abbey for six hundred years before their line broke and the estate became the school. The last bust by the door was of Headmaster Byrne. Charley reached and felt behind the cold face, running his fingers through a sheet of dust. He grasped the long shaft of the key and slipped it in his pocket.

Running his fingers over the heavy iron-bound slats of the front door, he felt his way around the room to the North Wing and the long hall of masters' chambers. Thin beams of light shone from under some doors, sending pale daggers of illumination across Charley's path. The splashes of light across the carpet made the faded pattern look like shifting desert sands.

He stepped softly and slowly, testing each floorboard under the threadbare carpet that ran down the center of the hall. To each side, he heard the rumbling of snores or the shuffling of papers, the crisp flap of a stiff page turning. He stepped toe-to-heel, inching his way down the hall.

At last, he reached the double doors at the end. No light shone under the door; no sounds echoed from behind it.

Charley pulled the key from his pocket. He brushed his fingertips over the door in front of him, finding the cold keyhole. He slipped the key in and turned it, muffling the noise with the front of his sweater.

Moonlight shone through the high windows behind the empty desk. Charley crept inside and shut the door behind him, dropping the key back into his pocket.

The massive desk had few drawers. One was full of parchment scraps and pen nibs, plain envelopes scattered through the mess. The bottom drawer held a stack of dusty ledgers and a bottle of foul-smelling spirits.

Behind the tall desk chair, below the windows, stood a chest of drawers. The drawers' paper labels read "A-H," "I-P," "Q-Z," "Retired."

Charley pulled at the top drawer. A long row of dark envelopes rolled out, each with a last name printed at the top in pencil. Charley thumbed through them. No Bowles. He rolled the drawer closed.

He pulled at the bottom drawer marked "Retired." It stuck fast. A small keyhole gaped below the label. Charley let out a long breath, stirring a cloud of dust. He turned back to Byrne's desk and went through the drawers again, feeling deep into the corners, opening each box of pen nibs, careful to set things back as they were.

He checked the books and shelves next. Careful not to leave a trail in the dust, he gently touched the top edge of each book near the desk. At last, he found one: solid wood instead of pages, bound in a frayed cloth cover labeled *The Secret of Man*. His father had something similar stored in his trunk. He remembered the day his father had shown him the secret, and the small treasures hidden inside.

He'd thought of his father as a grand adventurer in that moment. He couldn't think the same of the headmaster. Byrne's secrets were altogether too sinister. Charley opened the box.

A collection of letters tied with a tattered strip of blue ribbon, a scented handkerchief, and a ring of small keys lay tucked inside. Charley took the keys to the chest of drawers and tried each of them until he finally heard the mechanism release.

Inside were more brown envelopes, their names erased. Charley flipped through them, two dozen in all, each one battered and empty, the rubbed-out names indistinguishable.

Charley took the envelope from the top of the pile and held it up in the moonlight, studying the faint depression in the label. *It might have been "Bowles,"* he thought. *It's the right shape and length for the word.* He took it to the desk.

He removed a thin sheet of paper from the drawer and laid it against the envelope, over where the name had been written. He took a pencil from the case on the desk and lightly brushed the lead over the thin paper. "Bowles" appeared, faintly, highlighted in the field of graphite. Charley folded the slip of paper and put it in his pocket.

He put the empty envelope back in place, closed and locked the drawer, and returned the keys to the hidden box, tucking them under the packet of letters.

A mumbling came from behind the side door. Charley froze, the heat of rapid heartbeat rising up his neck. He dropped behind the desk and crawled under it, into the large space carved out for the headmaster's legs. He pulled the chair closer, blocking himself in.

The side door opened. Feet scuffed across the carpet. Charley peered under the desk and watched as veined ankles shambled across the floor. He saw the hem of a nightgown sway by the chair, and a gnarled hand pulled open the bottom drawer. He heard the clink of glass, the slosh of liquid, and the smell of spirits tickled his nose. He pinched it, trying not to sneeze.

The old hand dropped the bottle back into the drawer and pushed it closed. The shuffling feet retreated across the carpet. The side door closed.

Charley waited. His feet began to tingle with sleep as he crouched silently beneath the desk. A grunting snore sounded from the room. He pushed the chair away and climbed out from under the desk. He headed for the double doors.

A flash of white caught his eye, in the fading glow of coals in the hearth.

Bending down, Charley saw scraps of paper in the grate, mixed in with wood ash. He plucked them out of gritty piles. Bits of writing showed on the small pieces, but the words themselves were long burned away. Charley dropped them back into the ash and turned back to the door.

Moonlight reflected off the glass surfaces of the pictures surrounding the door. Charley moved closer, twisting his neck till he could see through the glare to the figures in the pictures. In the oldest two—the ones with the first students, for whom the school was new, born of the old earl's empty legacy—he saw the previous matron, staring out at the camera with wide, challenging eyes. She had the same wild hair as the gardener, the same delicate but hooked nose over full lips, though she was pale where he was dark, as his father must have been. He wondered which of the boys had occupied the hack seat. Which of them had run—or vanished.

Charley reached up and took down the picture. He held it against his chest and pulled the sides of his cardigan closed over it.

The hall outside the tall doors was darker. Fewer lights shone from beneath the masters' doors, and the light that was there had grown dim in the way of unattended fires.

He pulled the door closed and locked it, then tiptoed carefully back down the long corridor to the entry hall and replaced the key behind the bust of Byrne. He listened for the tap-tap of the night master's shoes. Silence. He crept back down the north hall, past the entrance and dining hall and into the South Wing, through the kitchens, to the servants' stairs.

At the second-floor landing, he heard the fall of a foot on the stairs behind him, around the curve of the tower. He climbed more quickly, lightly, on the balls of his feet. The steps behind him shuffled after, slow but gaining.

Charley leapt into the hall on the second floor, and saw the glow of the master's lantern ahead, the tap-tap advancing down the hall toward him, the scuffling shuffle behind.

He edged along the wall. His head whipped back and forth, till his hand brushed against the closet door to his side. He pulled it open and dashed inside. The tap-tap and glow passed by. When it faded, the shuffling grew nearer.

Charley crouched down, clutching the edge of the picture beneath his sweater, its edges digging into his fingers. He felt the loose board slip against his back. He caught it as it tipped and leaned it against the wall. A draft blew from the dark tunnel beyond, carrying the sweet smell of old blood.

The shuffling stopped outside the closet door. The handle rattled and began to turn.

Charley darted into the blackness of the tunnel and ran.

CHAPTER FOUR

Ten steps into the dark space, Charley hit a wall and his feet slid in gravelly dust, slipping sideways over the edge of a stair to his left. He caught himself against the rough beams of the inner wall and fled down the stairs, trailing his hand over the splintered wood and crumbling stone around him.

The stairs pitched steeply down the narrow tunnel. His shoulders scraped against the walls as his feet pounded thick slabs of unfinished wood that bowed in the middle, sagging with age—wide timbers from when Britain still had ancient forests, like in the stories his father told.

The loose plank rattled behind him. Something slid through the grit at the top of the stairs.

Charley abandoned all hope of silence and threw himself forward through the dark. The stairway pitched steeply down, and the air around him cooled and dampened. He landed on rough packed earth layered over gritty brick. A faint trickle of water echoed through the tunnel. The smell of wet dust tickled his nose.

He reached out for a wall—compacted clay, slick with mineral deposits, freezing to the touch—and he ran, scraping his fingers through the damp earth. He couldn't hear the shuffling behind him any longer, only the slow flow of water and the echo of his own footfalls, pounding and crunching on the ancient bricks of the tunnel floor.

The wall bent and curved away from his hand, and he steered his feet to follow. His mind raced as he tried to orient himself. The back wall of the closet faced east, the same as his dormitory window. The left turn would have taken him north. Now he curved to the right, but how far? The angles and trajectories were lost in haste and disorienting darkness.

I'm under an old church, he thought. *Perhaps this is a catacomb, or an escape tunnel for persecuted Catholics.*

He shivered and slowed his pace, clutching at a cramp in his side. *I don't think staff have been using these tunnels.*

The floor began to slope upward. Charley's thighs strained; his legs shook as he pressed his feet to the floor, climbing the underground hill.

His foot thunked against a plane of wood. He reached out and felt the square edges of another set of stairs. He held the picture to his chest and climbed, panting, the moist cloud of his breath surrounding his face in the cold, closed space.

Brick dust scraped and crumbled behind him, distant but steady, growing nearer through the tunnel.

Charley hung his head. He took a deep breath and began to run again, steadying himself against the wall.

The wall changed from clay to wood as he ascended, planks set into stone, the interior structure of another wall. He reached a flat landing. Stairs continued to his left. A crack of light leaked through a gap around a crooked board in the wall. He pressed against it and it fell away, rattling against the floor of a dusty corridor enmeshed in webs. The dim light of dawn fought through grimy windows around planks of wood nailed across panes of broken glass.

Charley squeezed through the opening and pushed the plank

back in place. To his right, a curving set of servants' stairs twisted away, up and down. Across from him, down the long hall to his left, a row of closed doors faced the tall broken windows. The ceiling hung with curtains of cobweb swaying in slow currents of stale air.

He pulled a dusty strand of web from the wall and rolled it between his fingers.

"*Theridiidae*," he whispered, his breath blowing flecks of dust from the old web. He scanned the walls for the bead-black bodies spotted with yellow, their front legs long and hooked. Nothing moved in the silent hall.

Thick layers of dust muffled his footfalls, and revealed the dragging tracks of other feet that had walked this way. The tracks led to and from each door in the hall, back and forth from the twisting staircase.

There was a stirring in the wall behind him. It paused on the other side of the loose plank. Charley backed silently away from the hidden passage. The board twitched. He turned and sprinted up the spiral stairs. *I must be on the second floor, heading to the third.*

The steps here were raw stone, worn smooth and low in the center over centuries. The soft leather of his slippers was silent against the stone, but he noticed the addition of his own tracks to those already left in the accumulated dust. He tried to step where tracks already existed, but didn't dare slow his speed.

The stairs leveled to a wide landing. To his right stretched another hall lined with closed doors. Above him, the staircase continued—narrower, the steps more worn. The hallway was washed clear and warped with rain from the high row of broken windows, their board coverings long since rotted and fallen away. At the end of the hall, a large carved door sagged on its ancient hinges. Weak light crept in around its edges.

Charley stared at the floor between him and the bright doorway. Was this the floor Malcolm had glimpsed, rotten and likely to cave under his feet? The dragging tracks continued through the dust on the floor, from door to door along the length of the hall, but none crossed the threshold of the wide oak door.

He stepped into the hall, eyes locked on the scrap of light. Before he could breathe again, he was eye-to-eye with a carved wooden face staring out from the warped panel. He couldn't tell, through the veil of web and dust, if it was a man's face or a demon's.

Charley bent to the wide triangular gap that the fallen door exposed along the floor.

He could tell that the room beyond had once been opulently furnished. A tall four-poster bed sat against the wall, trailing dark drapes to a floor scattered with broken stones and splintered boards.

Charley squeezed through the space at the bottom of the door. He knew he was leaving traces in the dust, but he also knew that the slouching, aged figure could never pass through the small opening—and clearly hadn't ever tried, for as long as the dust had been collecting.

The framed picture pressed into his chest as he slid across the floor. He wriggled, pushing with his toes and pulling with his fingertips, till he was in the old bedchamber.

As he stood, he could see the source of the weak light was a jagged hole in the stone wall, crudely sealed with rotting wooden planks. Stones were missing from the floor around the planks. Dry ivy crept up through the hole that dropped, dizzyingly, three stories to the grounds below.

Charley edged along the wall away from the door, afraid to step out into the center of the room.

A moving figure caught his eye and a shout escaped his throat. The figure's mouth gaped. A mirror. He had stepped in front of a small dressing table. His rapid breath shook the delicate tracery of web that veiled the scattered artifacts on its surface. Charley reached out a shaking hand and brushed the dust-feathered web away from the table.

Pearl pins and shell combs lay cluttered around a boar-bristle brush. Charley's heart constricted. He hadn't seen things such as these since his mother had them. He remembered sitting on a pillow and watching her pull a brush like this through her hair. He remembered her plucking the loose strands from the brush. He remembered finding them in the house long after she had died.

The dusty brush on the table was matted with fine hairs. Some were dark, but most shone silver in the faint light. *Did all this belong to the earl's lost wife? Was this her room?*

Charley backed away from the table and eyed the rubble scattered across the floor, the long ancient boards across the far wall. *This is the collapse. This is where she died. This is why the East Wing is sealed.*

Charley's heel struck the wooden door. He pressed himself against it as though the weight of all that missing stone had settled in his chest. He lowered to the floor and squeezed through the opening, back out into the hallway and away from the room. The pressure in his chest eased.

It was as if the room was frozen in time. His father hadn't kept his mother's things laid out as if she were coming back for them. As if they'd do anything but decay, like everything else she'd left behind. He'd given them to Charley's nurse before they left. She had wept and slipped the yellow linen scarf around Charley's neck when he'd kissed her goodbye.

The groan of ancient beams called him back to the present. He shook his head clear. *It's like the dust here is made of memory. You could wander in the past for years.*

He ascended the spiral stairs again, up into the narrower, darker part. At the top, under the sloped eaves of the servants' attic, stretched another hall, this one with only a few small windows and narrow doors. Dark stains covered the sagging floors and ate away at the plaster on the walls. The whole hall smelled rancid, its air close and ill-ventilated. The small glass windowpanes were buried deep into thick beams set in stone, un-opening and covered in a veil of fly-studded lace web. The air hummed with the vibrations of small wings.

In the largest of the rooms, at the center of the hall, was a small hearth nearly filled with a large iron pot. A septic soup pooled at the bottom. As Charley leaned over it, he felt warmth on his face. He reached out a hand. The pot was still hot. The embers beneath it still glowed dimly with residual heat. Beside the hearth was a basket like the one he'd seen in the kitchens, full of bread crusts and meat rinds, potato peels and carrot tops. Flies swarmed the basket, which let off a stink like a midden heap.

Someone is living here...eating. He looked at the sticky stains on the floor. *Someone here is bleeding.*

He needed to get out, away from the shuffling figure and back to Sam. Charley backed from the room and retreated to the stairs, this time hurrying around and around, hoping the first floor might offer a new route of escape.

The stairs ended in a long, dark hallway. The floor was thick with an ancient rug, the walls blanketed with old tapestries. Both were blackened and scorched in places, as if they had long ago stifled their own fires.

At the end of the hall was another pair of large carved doors like the ones to the lady's chamber, etched deep with floral lattices and twisted faces. These hung straight, shut fast.

Just beyond the closed doors, the hall ended in a brick wall. Charley rested his hand against it. On the other side would be the entrance hall, the foyer with its rows of busts and sweeping staircase. Another world.

The brickwork was covered in jagged scratches. Flakes of brick crumbled away from his touch and gathered in dusty piles on the floor.

A moan sounded beside him, and something slammed against the wooden doors.

Charley screamed and ran for the stairs.

One of the tapestries bucked and rippled against the wall. Charley darted into the twisting staircase and climbed.

He rushed into the second-floor hallway. He didn't want to go back into the tunnel. He went to the first door and tried the knob. It was locked, as was the next. The third door opened.

It was a dormitory room, identical to his own, but hobbled together from bits of broken furniture. Eight bent and broken bed frames, four to each side, lined the long walls. Small tables sat between them. A closet stood at the end, near two dilapidated chests of splintered wood drawers, and a crumbling bookshelf half-full of dark, mildewed books.

The mattresses were moth-eaten, with straw, sawdust, and grey cotton spilling across moldy, threadbare blankets. Pillows dotted with dark stains, feathers pouring through holes, lay rumpled at the head of each bed.

Rotten toes of old leather shoes poked out from under the rusty bed frames. Dusty, tattered jackets hung over the posts. It was his room—if it had been forgotten for an age.

Every dull surface sucked light from the room, the dust and grime soaking it up. A small glint of light sparkled at the far end, reflecting the glow sneaking between the boards across the fractured window.

Charley walked through the room to the sloping table between the two beds at the end of the row. There on the table sat Bowles' crystal, the clear spires branching out of the grey rock. Charley's hand shook as he reached out and picked it up, its points poking into his skin, the rough rock of its curved base scraping against his dry, dirty palm.

He looked down to the bed—what would have been Bowles' bed in their room. The ratty blankets were rumpled over the grey mattress, the pillow speckled with red. Charley's chest felt tight, his breaths rasping as he pushed them out of his throat. He put the crystal in his pocket.

He pressed against the boards across the window, but they held. The wood felt soft, but twisted nails still pinned it firmly to the walls.

He peeked into the hall. It was empty. The loose board to the tunnel passage was still set in the plaster. The hair on his neck rose at the thought of its squeezing dark, of what might be waiting in there for him. He ran to the servants' staircase and climbed up, around, and out into the third-floor hall. The floorboards twisted and tipped under his feet, pitching him toward the open windows where the boards had blown away. If this was how Malcolm had gotten in, then this was where Charley could get out. He leaned out over the stone window frame. The cresting sun shone across the small flood of water covering the grass far below.

The bell sounded for morning. Soon, boys and masters would stream out of their rooms, filling the halls and yard.

Charley looked down. The rough-hewn grey bricks of the abbey walls stood out at odd angles all the way down to the lawn.

He took the picture from under his sweater and clamped his teeth over its narrow frame. His teeth sank into the soft wood, filling his mouth with the bitter flavor of flaking gold varnish. He swung one leg out the window, then the other, turning, gripping a stone with his toes. His slippers fell, tumbling, banging against the stone wall before landing with a splash in the soggy grass.

He clutched the windowsill and lowered himself, digging his bare toes between freezing stones, gripping with his fingertips. He pressed himself against the building, humming through his clenched teeth, his breath fogging the glass of the picture.

A growling cough sounded above him. He looked up just in time to see a grey shock of matted hair vanish from over the windowsill.

Charley climbed faster. He heard splashing below but dared not look down.

"Charley? Charley, what are you doing?" Sam's voice called up to him.

He'd reached the second-floor row of windows. He rested, standing on the ledge. The wooden board nailed over the opening crumbled against his hand. He continued to climb.

"Careful, Charley. I'm here if you fall." Sam stood beneath him, arms outstretched.

Charley's head spun. He breathed deep. He felt his grip weaken, but lowered himself, carefully, until he felt the wide hands of the gardener at his ankles, then knees, then gripping his waist. He fell away from the wall, leaning back into Sam's arms. Sam lowered him to the grass. The icy water stung his feet.

"What in hell's name d'you think you're doin', climbin' the building like a mad spider! You could have…" Sam froze. He pulled the picture from Charley's mouth and wiped the breath-fog away with his sleeve.

Charley stood, panting, hands on his knees, staring up at the empty window he'd climbed from.

Sam stared at the photograph. "That's her," he said.

Charley nodded. "Better hide it. I took it from the headmaster's wall."

Sam gaped at him, his eyes wide. He tucked the picture under his jacket. "I'd better go get the key," he said, "and you'd better run back t' your room. I'll meet you after dinner, in the greenhouse." He jogged away, clutching at his chest, splashing rippling waves across the flooded lawn.

Charley pulled on his damp slippers and ran for the door.

* * *

Charley coughed and sneezed through breakfast, his mucus grey with the dust and dirt running from his nose. His eyes swelled red at the rims.

"Charley, you'll kill us all with that plague. Why don't you go to the infirmary and get some rest?" Malcolm's voice was harsh, but he helped Charley stand.

Matron Grace sent him to bed, excusing him from classes for the day.

In the washroom, while the other boys sat in class, Charley drew a hot bath, scrubbed his face and hair, dug the clay of the tunnel from beneath his fingernails, and removed his dirty bandage, running water over the red seam of flesh.

The bathwater turned a disconcerting grey-brown as he scraped the dirt and fear-sweat from his pores in a dark paste. Charley drained the tub, filled it again, scrubbing till the water came away clean. He sighed and let the light from the window wash over him. The East Wing had left a shadow in his thoughts that stained his mind. No amount of soap or light touched it. *What else is hidden there?*

He stuffed his nightclothes and sweater into his numbered laundry bag, along with the shirt he'd pulled on for breakfast. He buried the crystal and the crumpled paper in his tack box. Sweat and grime had washed the graphite across the hidden word, obscuring it completely. The name 'Bowles' had disappeared as completely as the boy had.

He took the back stairs to the kitchens. The staff flew left and right, darting between steaming pots and glowing ovens.

Charley asked a passing kitchen girl for a cup of broth. She brought it and he sipped, perched on a chair in the corner, watching the warm frenzy of the staff. His gaze drifted to the flagstones beneath their feet. He wondered if any of them knew what lay just beyond their pantry shelves.

He left his empty cup on his chair and walked down the long hall, out the solid main doors, crossing the grass to the greenhouses on the southwest lawn.

Sam was inside, sitting on an upturned bucket and staring vacantly at the floor as he crumbled clods of dark earth between his fingers. He looked up when Charley latched the door behind him.

Charley turned over another bucket and sat next to him in the narrow aisle between rows of raised beds.

The air clung to Charley's face, thick and damp, a warm contrast to the brisk air outside. A pervasive glow filtered through the foggy, sanded glass as beads of water ran down its slanted panes. It smelled of green things growing against the seasonal scripture of nature.

Sam lifted himself a bit, tipped the bucket, reached under, and pulled the photograph from beneath it. He'd removed it from its frame, revealing more of the picture and a captioned list of names.

"That's her, Charley," he said, lightly running his earthy finger over the image of the crisp, severe matron. "Miss Eleanor Ward, it says here. She was Ellie Forster t' me and dad. She wasn't anything to the twins." His face pinched in on itself. Soft sighs passed his lips, tears carving tracks through the dirt on his face.

Charley put a hand on his shoulder. Sam leaned into the touch and cleared his throat. "Thank you, Charley," he said, sliding the photograph back under the bucket. "Was tha seen last night? How did you end up on the wall outside the East Wing?"

"I don't think I was seen," Charley said. "It was too dark. But someone was following me. It was that same shuffling step I've heard in my room at night, the one that moved Bowles' bed and broke my jars. The grey figure Malcolm calls a ghost." Charley pulled at the fringe of his scarf. "He was behind me, and I saw the night master's light ahead, so I ducked into the closet. The thing that followed me—he started to open the closet door, so I ran through the space behind the wall. He knew the tunnel was there, too. He followed me in, chased me through a passage that ran under the school, through stairs in the walls. When I came out through another wall, I was in the East Wing.

"There was a room there, set up just like ours, only with old broken beds and rotten sheets. I found Bowles' rock on the table, the one that went missing the night he did. It was there, just where he'd kept it in our room. I took it. I was too afraid to go back, to follow the tunnel again, and the thing was still after me. So I climbed out the window."

Sam stared. Charley looked down. He picked up a damp twig from the floor and stirred the dirt.

"But did you see owt of who it was that followed you?"

"No. I saw grey hair for just a moment in the window. It was too dark in the tunnels to see anything. I just heard it, the scraping step, and a cough." Charley felt a tickle in his throat as he thought back to the dusty room. "It looked like someone was sleeping there, in that room. The sheets were mussed. There was blood on the pillow."

They sat in silence for a moment. Sam's fists clenched and relaxed rhythmically.

"Did you find an address? Anything in th' headmaster's office besides the picture?"

Charley shook his head. "There was a stack of empty files in a locked drawer, and bits of paper in the hearth. Whatever information he had there is gone."

Sam rubbed his chin, scrubbing dirt from his hand into the coarse hairs of his beard. "I doubt there's owt t' be found, then. Odd that he'd destroy the file. I know most old files are kept, stored in boxes above th' old carriage house." He looked at Charley.

"Sam, I don't think Bowles ran away."

"I don't know what t' think, Charley, but I'm beginning to fear you might be right." Sam rubbed at his eyelids.

"I don't think we can tell the headmaster," Charley said.

"Definitely not, no." Sam broke apart more clods of dirt, dropping the loose soil into a clay pot.

"Is there anyone else here that we can trust?"

"I don't know, Charley."

"Matron Grace was very kind to me and Bowles when he was hurt," Charley said.

Sam nodded, his thick eyebrows raised. "I heard her arguing with th' headmaster once, about proper diet and medications for students. She didn't sound too pleased with him. She's the one who commissioned that big vegetable patch."

"She sent me to bed sick this morning and excused me from classes. I'll go visit her and see if she can help."

Sam rose and carried his pot of loose soil to a flowerbed, dumping the rich earth over a fresh plot. "Be careful, Charley. Whatever it is tha's onto, it's not something tha was meant t' know." Sam's voice broke, and he turned his back.

Charley nodded and left the greenhouse, the sound of clay pots shattering behind him as he ran across the lawn.

The matron wasn't in the infirmary when he arrived. He sat on the bed where Bowles had slept and looked across the room, out the pointed-arch windows at dark winter clouds moving in.

* * *

"Charley?"

He saw his mother in the garden at their house in Cape Town. Her straw hat brushed the low-hanging leaves of lemon trees, filling the air with fresh, tangy oils. She called to him from the shade, smiling, her cheeks rose-pink, before the red of fever ravaged them. He breathed the smell of her skin as he cried into the soft linen scarf wrapped round her neck.

"Charley, are you okay?"

He started. He opened his eyes. A woman stood over him. His heart raced with confusion, elation, till he realized it wasn't his mother, but Matron Grace. He wasn't home. His mother was long gone, her bones far away.

"Are you feeling all right?" she asked.

Charley sat up from the bed, wiping a film of sweat from his upper lip.

"Sorry," he said. "I was waiting for you. I didn't mean to fall asleep."

She put her hand to his forehead. "You don't have a fever. Is your cough worse?"

"No, I'm fine, really. I…" His eyes darted, searching for the right questions.

"Let me make us a cup of tea," she said, and went to her kettle. She clicked a switch, and a blue flame shot out of the pipe under the burner.

"Matron Grace, do you happen to have Bowles' gran's address, in London? I'd like to write to him, but I don't know where to reach him."

"I'm sorry, Charley, I don't have it. The headmaster will, though. Perhaps you should check with him." She poured steaming water into two cups and dropped tin balls of tea leaves in each.

"I would, but…I'd rather he not know I was writing at all."

She stirred sugar into the tea and brought a cup to Charley. She balanced her cup on her knee as she sat on the bed next to his. The water in her cup swirled, the honey color darkening to rich amber.

"Perhaps I'll ask him for it myself. I think it would be reasonable for me to inquire after his injury, as I was the one who treated it." She raised her cup to her lips and tipped it, peering at Charley over the rim.

"I would be very relieved to have news. Thank you."

They drank their tea in silence.

Charley stood to leave. "Thank you for the tea, and for asking after Bowles. And for the time to rest today, as well."

"Of course, Charley. As for the rest, you look like you could use more of it. Hold on a moment." She walked to her desk in the corner and pulled out a small piece of paper and a pen. She scrawled a note and handed it to Charley. "A leave note, in case you feel ill again or have trouble sleeping. You have permission to visit the infirmary at any hour." She smiled and pointed to the narrow door by the fireplace. "My room's just through there. Knock if you need me."

"Thank you, Matron."

"Take care, Charley. I'll let you know when I hear back from Bowles, how he's doing—and I'll give you the address."

Charley thanked her again, dipped his head, and left, the pass tucked into his jacket pocket, and the scent of his mother still swimming in his thoughts.

* * *

Back in the dorm, the boys were reading and playing games. They ignored Charley as he stepped around them, over rings of marbles and magazines lined up for trade, except for Sean, who tried to trip him with his bandaged foot. The gauze had soaked through with blood and pus—the old wound split back open every time he gave in to the pull of the pitch, against Matron Grace's orders.

Charley sat down in front of his tack box and lifted the lid. He pulled out the jar of common black ants he had collected and watched them swarm over a piece of biscuit he'd dropped in the day before. They scaled the morsel, pried at it with their mandibles, and carried a piece down to join the marching line circling the perimeter of the jar, their pheromone trail an infinite loop, sweet treasure hoisted high.

"Shall we look forward to those 'beauties' in our bed sheets next?"

Charley turned. Malcolm stood over him. "Master Brown said you were ill today," he said.

"I've just come back from the infirmary. I'm fine, though. Must have caught a draft, is all," Charley said. He cleared his throat.

"I'm glad to hear you're fine," Malcolm said.

"Thank—"

"It's easy to catch a draft out of bounds at night."

Charley paled. He'd forgotten the mound of clothes he'd hidden under his blanket, to fool the night master's prying lantern. It wouldn't have fooled Malcolm's closer inspection.

"The yard's been flooded and our shoes are a mess." Malcolm, Mullins, and the others laughed as Malcolm dropped a pair of muddy shoes in Charley's lap.

Charley lifted them and set them aside. They were wet inside and out, spattered with mud and foul-smelling.

"Still, nothing better than a football match in the mud; wouldn't you agree, Charley?"

"I wouldn't know, sir," Charley said.

"I know you wouldn't. So where were you last night?" Malcolm's face grew serious, the humor sliding off like rain rolling down the window.

"I wasn't feeling well," Charley said. He pulled the paper from his jacket pocket. "I went to the infirmary. Matron Grace told me to come back tonight if I need."

Malcolm scrutinized the paper. He held it back out to Charley, who had to pull it from his pinched fingers.

Sean stared at the pass as Charley folded it and placed it in his pocket. He'd have to sleep with it on his person, he realized. His face burned under the pressure of the greedy eyes boring through him.

Malcolm turned his shoulder and walked back to his bed. "If you're too weak to polish, we completely understand," he said, his voice dripping with the implication that what they understood was his weakness, and they weren't empathizing.

Sean pulled his shirt up over his head and moaned like a ghost at Charley.

Charley turned his back on the spreading laughter. He pulled a stack of rags from the cupboard. The rest of the boys dropped their shoes beside him and went to their tea, leaving Charley with his thoughts and the smell of polish and sweaty insoles.

* * *

Headmaster Byrne took a long drink from his bottle and felt the lines in his face, creased where the whisky once made him wince.

He placed the tip of his finger into the cupped palm of the small china doll on his desk. He took another drink and brushed one of the doll's curls behind its delicate ear. *So much like her*.

He shook his head and stood, turning to the tall stack of file drawers behind his desk. He pulled a file from a low drawer and dumped its contents onto his desk. He rubbed out the file's label and set it aside. The pages stared back at him from the cluttered pile. *This one will be easier than most. So little family, so far away.* The doll stared at him, her glass body propped against the tall wooden telephone stand.

He tore the pages into long strips, then the strips into small squares, then carried the squares to the fire and scattered them over the coals. The dim glow of deep embers began to catch and the fire grew, heating his face even more than the whisky had.

He started to sweat, and stepped back into the center of the room. His gaze traveled to a spot on the wall—his favorite spot—and he gasped. An angry shout gurgled up from his gut. The picture was gone.

Choking on his rage, on the whisky-flavored bile that fought up his throat, he ran to his bedchamber and pulled the tasseled cord by the bed.

Who was in my rooms—who could have taken that picture—who could have known to take that *picture…?*

A fist tapped at his door. "Headmaster?"

"Enter!" he called.

Master Brown stepped into the office. "Did you need something, Byrne?"

"Yes, Brown. Who was in my rooms today? I must know immediately."

"No one that I know of, sir. The maids, I suppose. Shall I check your appointments?"

"Yes, do. Something has been taken."

Master Brown gaped. His gaze slipped to the desk behind the headmaster.

Byrne collected himself. "Nothing valuable. I'm sure it was just misplaced. But I must have an answer, of course."

"Of course, sir. I'll continue my rounds and make inquiries first thing."

"Thank you, Brown."

The master slipped out the door.

Byrne turned to his desk. The doll lay slumped against his

writing pad, tumbled from where she had sat. The heat of the fire, of the whisky, drained from his face. He picked up the small glass figure, pinched its small hand in his fingertips, and carried it to his bedchamber.

So like her.

* * *

Matron Grace breathed into the damp linen stretched across her mouth and nose. She tasted copper, the bitter tang of metals and astringent. Her hand hovered in a cloud of blue steam as she tipped the vial into the beaker bubbling on her hotplate. The steam turned ash-brown as the liquids boiled together, leaving a ring of dark residue at the high-level mark.

Grace turned down the heat and gripped the beaker in metal tongs wrapped in wool. She set it on a cast-iron trivet to cool and moved her kettle to the hotplate.

She pulled the wet strip of linen down below her chin and turned. She shrieked as her face met a line of buttons blanketed in black robes. Hands gripped her shoulders.

"Silence, Grace."

She gulped breath—tasted the fumes of her mixture in the air. "I'm sorry, Headmaster. I didn't know you were there. Would you like tea?"

Byrne looked at the sticky, steaming beaker. "No, thank you. I came to ask you a question."

"Yes, sir?"

"Master Brown says you stopped by my office earlier. Did you, by any chance, remove a picture from my wall?"

"What? No, of course not."

"Grace." His eyes grew wild. "Are you quite certain?"

Her eyes met his. Her nerves stiffened into resolve. "Of course I'm sure." Her lips thinned, chin jutted forward.

His eyes searched her face. "I'll be looking for it. If you see it, please make sure it's returned to me immediately."

"Which picture is it, sir?"

"You'll know it when you see it." He pulled the door shut forcefully behind him. The row of glass beakers rattled.

Grace strode to her mixtures, leaned over them, and breathed deeply. She pulled a small case of green glass vials from the cupboard and slipped a small tin funnel into one.

Her fingers trembled as she lifted the beaker and poured out a measure of thick liquid into each bottle.

* * *

Charley lay in bed, listening to the breathing of his roommates and the patter of rain against the window turning to the aggressive percussion of sleet.

He'd been lying still, hardly daring to breathe, for three rotations of the clunk-thunk of the on-duty master, his beam of light cast briefly in the room before moving on.

Charley waited. He knew the dusty, shuffling creature would come, knew that it must know that he'd been the one in the hidden tunnels, that he'd taken back Bowles' treasure.

When the master passed again, his steps growing slow as the hour grew late, Charley slipped out of his bed. He pulled the crystal from his tack box and set it on the bedside table where Bowles had placed it on their first night, where Charley had found it in the dusty twin room.

He rolled clothes under his blanket and crept to the front of the room. He stood against the wall to the side of the doorway, hand poised by the button for the electric lights.

Long minutes passed, and the master rounded the hall again, shining his light in the room. Charley held his breath, hoping the pile of clothes would stand their brief inspection again.

The master walked on, and in the silence of his wake, Charley heard it—the telltale shuffle.

It seemed more labored than before, slower, the dragging sounded heavier, burdensome. It advanced slowly down the hall.

He listened as it scraped, thumped, and dragged to the doorway. He smelled the dust of it as it paused in the hall. Heard a guttural whisper as it slid itself into the room. It went straight for the table with the crystal.

When it made its way there, Charley could see the outline against the window, against the moonlight reflected off the freezing rain.

It was no taller than Charley, hunched and wide, though Charley didn't know how much of its bulk was rotten rags. The gauzy bits hung from it in trailing tendrils, falling away from the frazzled shock of hair at its crown.

It grasped the crystal, raised it high in the air, and brought it punching down on Charley's pillow.

Charley froze. He clasped his hands over his mouth, trapping the scream there that choked him as it rose.

The figure raised the rock again and smashed it down with a force that shook the metal spindles of the bed frame.

Charley scrambled out of the room, no longer caring to see the murderous creature. He saw gauzy tendrils fly out as it spun toward his movement, heard the heaving drag as it pursued him, its ragged muttering harsh and enraged.

He ran for the central stairs, hoping to catch the master. He stumbled in the darkness, searching for a sign of the master's light. There was none.

He felt his way to the stairs, hooked his arm over the banister, lifted his feet, and slid down. His chest hit the newel post. He planted his feet on the tile floor and swung around the rail toward the back hall.

The infirmary door was open, a light glowing inside.

Charley raced in and closed the door behind him. He leaned against it, breathing heavily.

Matron Grace stood by her desk, a piece of paper in her raised hand. She, too, breathed heavily. She started and looked to Charley, then turned away.

Charley followed her gaze.

Headmaster Byrne stood by the hearth, his hand resting on the back of the chair where Bowles' head had been stitched. He stood right where the puddle of sick had landed.

Byrne straightened, his eyes flashing.

"What on earth are you doing here at this hour, young man?" He smacked his hand against the taut leather of the chair.

Charley gasped, then began to cough, looking to Matron Grace.

"He's been ill, sir. I asked him to come back tonight if his cough returned, so I could listen to his lungs. Do you have your pass, Charley?"

Charley reached into his pocket and pulled out the folded paper. The matron took it and held it out to the headmaster. He looked it over and handed it back to the matron.

"You see how our deeds come back to us, Charley? Sickness spreads. From mind to body and body to mind. I'll let you see to your charge, Matron."

Charley backed from the door as the headmaster opened it. The hall outside was empty, dark and silent.

"What's wrong, Charley?" Matron Grace asked, walking to the door and shutting it. "Is it your cough?"

Charley shook his head. His knees trembled. "I—I saw someone in my room. He chased me."

"Sit down, Charley. Let me bring you some tea."

Charley sat in the leather chair, drawing his legs up onto the cushion.

She worked at the burner. "Have you seen this person before, Charley? Did you recognize him?"

"I've seen him a few times, but I don't know him. In our room, before. Once, on the night that Bowles disappeared."

"The headmaster was just here about Bowles. I left him a note this afternoon, asking for the address. He came to tell me that the address he had was no longer in use."

"Oh," Charley said. His stomach tightened.

"When and where else have you seen this person, Charley, the one who was in your room?"

"Last night. I—I was out of my room at night, looking for something, and I heard the strange footfall behind me. I ran, and...I ended up in the East Wing. I didn't mean to," he said, as Matron Grace's hand rose to her mouth. "I got away through a window there, to the grounds. The gardener helped me down. I was afraid the man would come back tonight, and he did. I…took something from the East Wing. A rock that belongs to Bowles. This man, he tried to hit me with the rock, twice, hard." Charley couldn't lift his teacup. His hand shook.

The matron sipped her tea in silence, her eyebrows down.

"The footfall, Charley, the strange one—does it limp? Shuffle, like it's dragging something?"

Charley poured tea into his lap. "Yes!"

"I've heard that, too. Here in the infirmary. Also on the night Bowles left. Others have mentioned it before, in the past." She handed Charley a towel covered in dark stains.

He mopped at the tea in his lap. "Is it a staff member? Should we ask the headmaster?"

"I don't know him, if it is. I'll ask the housemaid if she has any staff with limps. Perhaps I can offer to help treat them. I don't think it's a good idea to ask the headmaster."

Charley nodded. "The other boys say he's a ghost. When I mentioned him to Master Brown, he said I was telling tales."

"Charley, I think it's best if you don't speak of this figure to anyone. This old abbey has its stories, but people will think you're mad."

"Do you mind if I tell Sam? The gardener? He's been helping me."

"Are you sure you can trust him, Charley? Headmaster Byrne said his mother was the matron before me." She shuddered and shook her head.

"Yes, I know she was. What do you mean?"

She looked at him, pursing her lips. "Never mind, Charley. But try to limit the time you spend with the gardener. It isn't seemly, in any case."

Charley set his cup on the table.

"Why don't you sleep here tonight?" She picked up his cup and carried it to the basin.

He hesitated.

"I'll lock the door. And I'll just be in my chamber, there."

Charley nodded. Exhaustion weighed heavy on him, his bones aching, his limbs like lead. He walked to the nearest bed and climbed in; the scent of soap rose from the stiff, cold linens. He watched a spider in the window, falling by her thread, hanging a net of web as if to catch the moon. He drifted into sleep.

CHAPTER FIVE

The morning bell rang, much quieter on the first floor than up near the tower in the dormitories.

Charley rubbed his eyes. The spider's web was complete, a mastery of interlocking strands arched across the tall window, catching the red morning sunlight in its fibers.

The matron moved quietly at the front of the room, as if she'd never left, the freshness of her stiff apron the only clue that she'd ever retired. Steam poured from the spout of the kettle on the burner.

Charley sat up. Matron Grace looked to him and smiled, then turned and poured the water into cups, bringing one to the stand at his bedside.

"You'd best go to your classes today. If I write you off again, they'll be coming by to confirm a grave illness."

Charley smiled and sipped his tea. The rim of his cup was chipped, and it snagged at his dry lips.

"I'll speak to the housekeeper first thing, at breakfast," she said. "Come by this afternoon and I'll let you know what I've learned."

"Thank you, Matron," Charley said, his voice rough with sleep.

He walked back to his room, the damp cold of morning soaking his bones as he went.

"In the infirmary again, our dear little invalid?" Malcolm asked.

Charley nodded, pulling pieces of uniform from his trunk.

"Did you get Sean sick on purpose, then? I hope he kept you up with his coughing."

Charley pulled on a sock. "I haven't seen him. Is he not well?"

Malcolm frowned. "You'd know better than I," he said. "He went to the infirmary just half after one this morning. Face burning like a coal."

Charley stared, sock half-drawn, hanging from his toes. "He never came to the infirmary," he said.

"He said he was. I saw him go." The other boys looked on. Some nodded. Malcolm hurried from the room, his face creased with worry. The boys stared at Charley, watched him finish dressing.

* * *

Charley fidgeted on the coarse wooden bench. He felt the splinters of it sticking to the wool of his trousers. The chaplain's voice jumped off the stone walls and tall windows, getting lost somewhere in the shadows of the high ceilings. Charley stared up past the thick beams and imagined he could see through the blanket of darkness to the arched stone buttresses and layers of wood, through the fine lattice structure of the ceiling as it became the floor of the next story. Through worn planks and threadbare carpets, through classrooms and rooftops and up into the sky.

He started as bodies shifted around him, all rising to sing. Charley hadn't heard what song had been chosen, but it didn't matter. He didn't know any of these songs, with their moaning organs and fluted voices. There was no power in a song without drums, though the priest clearly disagreed. No matter how hard he tried, he couldn't feel it.

The boys had left a space open for Sean a few rows ahead. It gaped now, like a missing tooth in a crooked grin.

Missing teeth. There were hundreds of them, just below their feet. *Maybe Sean went for whisky. Maybe he found the teeth. Maybe he got stuck below.* Charley felt his face tingle with the onset of lightheadedness. He needed to tell Malcolm, to ask if anyone had checked in the underground pantry. *In the crypt.*

He waited till the song swelled particularly loud, then leaned forward through a row of boys and hissed for Malcolm's attention. He didn't hear him. He leaned farther and tugged on the elbow of Malcolm's sleeve. Malcolm turned and scowled at him.

Charley pointed at the floor and raised his eyebrows. Malcolm frowned, shook his head, and turned back around. Charley growled in frustration. He needed to *speak* to him. He waited through another song and the summary of the lesson he was meant to have learned, the reading assignment he knew he wouldn't do. Finally, they were dismissed.

Charley pushed forward through the crowd that was now moving back against him, straining to get to Malcolm.

"What do you want, Winslow?" Malcolm took Charley's elbow and steered him through the crowd.

"Did anyone check the cellar? I mean, for Sean. Did they look where he goes for his whisky?"

"I looked myself. He wasn't there."

Charley's hopes dropped.

"I saw the tombstones, though." Malcolm's grip seemed to tighten around the joint of his arm. "You have a gift for finding trouble."

* * *

Dark clouds shrouded their morning exercise. A blanket of brown leaves covered the grass under the trees, their edges filigreed with ice. They crunched under foot as the rows of boys marched across the lawn.

Charley stood aside in the trees and lifted the leaves with a stick, searching out the creatures that sheltered from the onset of winter.

He'd constructed a fist-sized box from paper and paste, and he'd filled it with spiders and a new centipede. He'd filched jam jars from the kitchen, hidden them in his tack box, lids punctured, ready for his new wards. He hummed as he searched.

"That's a nice little tune." The gardener stepped softly across the damp leaves, bending, collecting fallen sticks and tucking them under his arm.

"Hello," Charley said, "I was hoping to find you."

"Tha won't find me under there," Sam said, laughing, nodding at the layers of leaves Charley had pulled back.

Charley grinned, but it faded quickly. "That man came back to my room last night. He tried to smash my head with a rock."

Sam leaned against a tree, his mirth melting away. "What did you do?"

"I ran to the infirmary. The matron let me sleep there with the door locked." He looked sideways at Sam. "She doesn't trust you, though."

Sam lifted his eyebrows and straightened. "I hardly know her. Not sure why she'd have an opinion either way."

"I think...it might have something to do with your mother. She mentioned her."

"I see." He shifted his load of sticks. "But she helped you."

"Yes. I told her what happened—what's been happening. She's already asked the headmaster for Bowles' address, and he claimed it wasn't good anymore. She's going to ask the housekeeper about the limping man. Ask if maybe it's a staff member." Charley handed Sam a stick. "She says she's heard it, too."

Sam shook his head. "Probably is a staff member. A cleaner or summat. Are you sure he was trying to hurt you, Charley?"

"Yes. And another boy from my room is missing."

Sam fumbled his load of sticks. "How d' you mean?"

"He got up last night to go to the infirmary, only he never arrived there. The door was locked. There was no knock. At least, none loud enough to wake me."

The gardener laid the sticks down at the base of a tree. "And what does th' headmaster say about that?"

"Nothing. I'm not sure anyone believes he's gone yet. He wasn't in the dormitory or infirmary—he never came to breakfast or chapel. I suppose he might have run off somewhere, only I know this thing was after me last night, chasing me through the halls where Sean would have been walking. And Sean's got a bandaged foot. He couldn't have run much."

Sam lifted his tweed cap and ran a hand across his forehead. "I think you're right, Charley."

"What are we going to do?"

"We need to get that lad's file afore they know he's really missing. It has to be now, before dinner for certain. If I was to get you the key again, would the matron help you? Would she distract th' headmaster long enow for you to take down the lad's information?"

Charley nodded. "I think she would, yes. I'm to meet her today."

"Good. I'll go get the key once classes start. I'll put it behind the second bust this time—the old earl."

"Thank you, Sam."

Sam straightened and picked up his bundle of sticks. He turned to the direction of the sheds and then stopped, turning back. "Charley," he said.

"Yes?"

"Best not tell the matron this was my idea." He walked over the soggy leaves, through the orchard to the row of old padlocked sheds.

Charley sprinted back toward the school. The bell rang. Charley cursed. He'd not have time to run back to his dorm before class. He placed the paper cube carefully inside his pocket; the scattering of delicate feet tickled his fingers through the paper. Locked together, his friends would battle through his lesson. His heart ached for his delicate charges, but he was anxious to learn which would win.

Seated at his desk, the rattle of insect legs against the paper box in his pocket seemed louder to Charley than the booming voice of Master Crawley. The rhythmic scurry of their fight for freedom made infinitely more sense than the Latin rattling off the professor's tongue.

"Winslow, are you listening?"

"I'm trying, sir."

The professor's heavy shoes beat against the thin carpet as he advanced on Charley's seat. "You're trying? Am I not speaking clearly?"

"Yes, sir. I just...I don't understand." Charley felt the paper box shake against his waist. The fight inside had begun in earnest. He flinched.

"What is the matter with you?"

"I'm not feeling well, sir." Charley felt the cricket beat against the paper cage, then the rattle of insects went silent. Charley sighed.

The boy next to Charley dove out of his chair. "He brought his damn bugs to class!"

Charley looked down. A stream of ants trickled from his pocket, carrying a struggling cricket.

Master Crawley stepped back and waved his robed arm. "Out! Get out of this room. Take those pests with you. And if you ever bring them into my class again, you'll be lashed on the spot."

Charley scrambled from his seat. He heard his small charges trampled against the floorboards behind him as he crossed the room.

"You're to spend the rest of the day in the hall."

Charley slipped out of the heavy door and into the corridor. He brushed the last few ants from his clothes and watched them carry their prize down the hall.

He sat against the wall and stared down the row of closed doors. Deep, muffled voices echoed from behind them, every bit as incomprehensible as from the room he'd just left.

He rested his head against the wall and ran his hands over the floorboards, looking for the familiar spots in the grain. He dug his fingernail deep into the wood, prying out splinters of the varnished floorboards, plowing furrows of patina, and awakening the bitter scent of old mop water. He'd worried at the same spot every time, digging the pit deeper, imagining he could dig all the way to Cairo. That he could find his father and go back to South Africa and their house on the cape, where his mother would be waiting in the garden with flowers in her hands and a jar of insects on the table.

The brazen bell woke him from his daydream. He looked down at the pit in the floor and saw it had filled with blood from a splinter wedged under his fingernail. He pulled the splinter out as he listened to hundreds of chairs scrape across the floor. Doors all along the hallway swung open and rivulets of boys poured into the hall, marching in lines out of one doorway and into another, like ants in underground tunnels. *I'm the cricket.* He pressed himself against the wall, willing himself smaller.

Master Crawley leaned out of the door next to him. "You are dismissed, Winslow."

Charley turned, marched thirty feet down the hall, and sat outside of another doorway. Behind it, his peers worried over mathematics. He began to dig at another pit in the floor.

When the morning's lessons had ended, when he reached the end of the hall, leaving a trail of pitted floorboards behind him, Charley stretched his legs and rushed toward the circling stairs, down to the infirmary.

Matron Grace was there, bent over the leather chair, pulling a long splinter from the finger of a young boy. Charley didn't know him; wondered if he, too, had spent the day in the hall worrying at the floorboards. Wondered where he'd dig to, if he could.

Charley waited, shifting his weight between his feet. When the boy was bandaged, Matron shooed him out, closing the door behind.

"Well," she said, "it's not one of the staff. The housekeeper said none of them walk with a lame foot, though from the way she said it, I'm sure she's heard it herself."

"Matron, I need your help. Again," Charley said.

"What's wrong, Charley?"

"I think another boy is missing—a boy from my room. Malcolm said he was coming here last night, but he never came by and he hasn't been seen since."

"Sean Mullin?"

"Yes, that's him."

She put her hand to her chest. "The headmaster came by asking about him earlier."

"I need to get into the headmaster's office before they know he's gone. I need to get his address before his file is destroyed, like Bowles'. I have a key, but I need a diversion."

The matron sat. "You have a key?"

Charley blushed. He nodded. "It was…left somewhere. I'll put it back, I promise. I just need to know—I need to be able to prove that boys aren't just running home, that they need help, something is happening to them—to us."

"It was you," she said.

"What?"

"You took the picture from the headmaster's office. He thought it was me."

"What? Why?"

"Never mind, Charley. I'll ask the headmaster to help me with something here in the infirmary. But don't take anything this time, promise me. You don't know what trouble you caused."

Charley hung his head. "I'm sorry. I took it for—for a friend. He had a relative who was here a long time ago. I promise—nothing this time."

Matron Grace raised her eyebrows. "Thank you for your promise, Charley. That's enough. When shall this ambitious deception occur?"

"As soon as possible. If you could have him join you here after lunch, I would have plenty of time."

"All right, Charley. I'll ask him here directly after lunch."

"Thank you, Matron." Charley gave her a small bow and left, hurrying to his study period. He'd have to spend it begging for notes again. Exchanging favors. He'd likely pass the time folding linens or polishing boots instead.

* * *

After study period, Charley followed the students filing through the halls to the dining room. He hung back and split off from the rest of the crowd at the bottom of the stairs, sneaking into the entryway. When the students and teachers were assembled inside and he heard the chaplain's booming voice saying grace, he crept out of his hiding spot and hurried to the second bust in the row lining the wall.

"Lord Ward, sixth Earl of Dunleigh", the plaque on the front read. A thought tickled the back of Charley's mind, but adrenaline washed away the sensation. He reached behind the marble statue and pulled out the key. He stuck it in his pocket and slipped through the entryway, behind the staircase and into the masters' corridor.

Most of the doors were closed, but a few stood open, spilling squares of light into the hall. The masters inside were no doubt taking their meals at their desks, anxious for solitude and a break from the throng of boys.

Charley crept down the hall. At the first open door, he peered through the hinge gap. The master inside browsed a bookshelf, his back to the hall.

Charley darted past.

The second master held a book to his face, and Charley hurried by.

Beyond the third door, a master sat staring forward into the hall, pen poised over paper. Charley watched and waited. Master Pullwick scrawled a few words and looked up again, rubbing an inky finger over his bushy white eyebrow, painting it indigo so that it appeared the youth of the other.

Finally, after a particularly long stare, an eternity to Charley, the master's crepe eyelids slid shut and a rumbling snore rose from him.

Charley burst past the door before the master could start himself awake, and sprinted down the remainder of the hall.

At the headmaster's door, he slid the key into the lock and turned it, pushed the door open, and closed it behind himself, locking it again from the inside.

He went straight for the file drawers and pulled open the one for letter M. He danced his fingers over the envelopes until he found "Mullins." Inside sat a collection of papers and forms. He pulled out the handful of papers and flipped through them—test scores, discipline records. All the standard forms and permissions signed by parents, medical records, and finally a contact sheet.

A metallic rattle sounded at the door. The handle turned.

Charley eased the drawer shut. He darted for the open door to the headmaster's chamber. Clutching the file to his chest, he slid under the tall bed just as the double doors pushed open.

"So sorry to have kept you waiting, I didn't realize anyone was—hello? Hello?" Headmaster Byrne walked around the office. Charley watched his feet traverse the rug, advancing toward the bedroom. "Is anyone here?"

Another set of black leather-shod feet walked through the door. The headmaster turned toward them.

"There's no one here," he said. He walked to the desk. "Have the maid bring my lunch. I'll get some things done and see if he comes back."

"Yes, sir," Master Brown's voice answered, and his shoes tapped out of the room.

Charley heard the gentle bell sound of the phone receiver being picked up.

"York, please." A pause. "Mullins, at Fairgrove." Another pause.

Charley shifted and glanced down at the sheet in his hand. Sean's family home was Fairgrove Manor in York.

"Mrs. Mullins, hello. This is Headmaster Byrne... Oh, goodness, no—Sean is doing quite well with his studies and athletics. Only I'm afraid he's fallen a bit ill, and I wanted your permission to have a physician from the village see to him... Of course, ma'am, I'll send for him at once. I just wanted to make it clear that the school will need to send you the bill for the service... Indeed, I didn't expect so, of course... Just a cough, ma'am, many of the boys have had it this season already. It's just a precaution, you understand. We don't take any chances with the treasures of Britain's future... Of course, thank you, ma'am, I'll call you directly when the physician has finished with his assessment. Good day." Another soft ring sounded as the earpiece was replaced.

Charley heard the chair scrape across the floor and Byrne grunting as he stood. Byrne walked to the fireplace, poured a bit of coal from a brass bucket, and stirred the fire. Charley saw a growing glow spread across the floor.

There was a weak knock at the door.

"Enter."

The tiny, slippered feet of a kitchen maid stepped in, crossing the carpet to the desk. There was a rattle of dishes on a tray. "Will there be anything else, sir?"

"No, thank you."

"Shall I return for any scraps, sir?"

"I'll ring if it's necessary. Dismissed."

The feet disappeared and the door swung shut.

Byrne walked back behind his desk. The rumble of drawer wheels on wood tracks sounded, followed by the quiet shuffle of paper. A pause and another shuffle.

"Dammit!" Byrne shouted and slammed the drawer.

The chair creaked and another drawer slid open. The clink of glass, a slosh of liquid. A loud glassy thump, then the drawer slid shut.

The dust under the bed was beginning to irritate Charley's nose and throat. He pressed his face into his sleeve, trying to filter out the particles.

Byrne tucked into his lunch, chewing noisily.

So, Sean is ill?

Charley wondered where he'd been hiding. Or, perhaps, finding the infirmary locked, he had gone to a master or a friend's room. Charley felt his face heat with shame. *What will Matron Grace say? Will anyone listen now? Just because Sean is safe, doesn't mean Bowles—*

There was a knock at the door.

"Enter," Byrne said around a mouthful of sandwich.

Malcolm walked in. Charley knew his shoes immediately—knew every stitch.

"Oh. I was expecting the gardener. I was told he wanted to speak with me about a boy causing trouble in the school at night. Is this about that?"

"Sir, I was coming to report that Sean Mullins did not attend his classes today."

"Ah, yes. I am aware of the situation, thank you, Malcolm. It will be seen to."

"Thank you, sir." Malcolm paused. "Is he...?"

"What?"

"Sir, is Sean all right? I haven't seen him since he fell ill."

"Oh, quite all right, I'm sure. How is that odd boy doing—the one with the insects? Is he settling in?"

"It's hard to say, sir. We rarely see him. He doesn't participate in exercises—spends his time outdoors hunting for bugs with the gardener—and he's often out of bed at night."

"I see. What a pity. I suppose I should have another word with him about the social benefits he's neglecting. Thank you, Malcolm. Here, take this away to the kitchens, please, boy."

Charley's throat tightened. Had the gardener complained of him? Was he the boy the gardener had mentioned? The dust under the bed made his eyes water. His nose and throat itched.

Malcolm left the room, carrying the headmaster's lunch tray.

Headmaster Byrne rifled through his files again, swearing, then stalked from the room in a huff.

Charley waited a few minutes, then slid out from under the bed. He straightened the file and placed it in the drawer, out of alphabetical order, hoping the headmaster would think it had just been misfiled.

He crept from the room and locked it.

Back in the entry hall, he replaced the key behind the earl's bust and walked to the infirmary. Matron Grace was there, folding bandages.

"Matron, may I visit Sean, please?"

"Charley! I'm surprised to see you back so quickly." She fluttered a bandage, dropping it. Charley picked it up and handed it to her. She brushed the dust from it and placed it in the basket. "What do you mean, visit Sean?"

Charley stared at her. Her face was flushed. "I suppose I was too quick to judge. I'm sorry I got you involved. I should have just gone to the headmaster, but..."

"Yes, the headmaster. He must not have received my note. He never came to pay me that visit. I was afraid for you and your plan, Charley. Did you make it okay? Did you get the address?" She twisted a bandage in her hands.

"I'm fine, yes, but is Sean not here? Headmaster Byrne said he was ill."

The matron's face blanched the color of her apron. "He's not here, Charley. He never has been. What a strange thing for him to have said."

Charley paled. "He's missing, then. And the headmaster isn't telling his parents…"

"What about his parents?"

"I better get back to the dorms. While I was hiding, I heard the head boy complain about me. I need to be more careful."

"Yes, Charley, you do. *Much* more careful. And you can begin by brushing the dust from your coat. You look just like…" She had destroyed the bandage in her hands. "Here." She handed him the ragged bandage.

He brushed his coat clean as he hurried back to the dorm, leaving a trail of dust behind him.

* * *

Malcolm stared at Sean's bed, at his rumpled blanket and pillow. He never did make up his bed properly, and Malcolm never could mete out the punishment for it. Not for Sean. They were practically brothers. He swallowed against the lump that grew in his throat. He couldn't shake the image of the headmaster, parading through the school, informing the staff that the boy couldn't be found. "Suspected of running away." Why would he go?

Malcolm climbed off the bed and knelt by Sean's tack box. He hesitated. He'd never exercised his right to search anyone's box before—that never sat right with him. But this was different.

He lifted the dented pine lid. The battered hinges rattled in protest. Inside the box was movement; a mound of shiny black pulsed in the bottom. Malcolm gasped. His face twisted in disgust. *Ants.*

A swarm of black ants coated a large pastry Sean had stashed away. No doubt a gift from his mother. The ants had plucked at it till it was half a pile of crumbs that they hauled in regiment lines through a crack at the back of the box.

Malcolm slammed the lid down. *We'll have to get this mess out of here.* He shook his head. *That stupid boy and his bugs.* Anger rose in him. He strode over to Charley's box and flipped open the lid.

Most of the bugs inside were dead—pinned out behind glass and labeled meticulously. Other bugs lay dead at the bottom of dirty jars. *There's something very wrong about that boy.*

Malcolm tugged at a cream-yellow scarf that had been tied around a smaller box. It came free and the box fell open. Dry, dead, giant beetles spilled across Malcolm's lap.

"Damn!" He picked them up by their curled legs and dropped them back into the box.

He saw a square of paper wedged under the lid. He pulled it free.

It was a photograph—a man in uniform with dark hair and a long mustache, his arm around the waist of a woman in a long summer dress, her fair hair piled in curls atop her head. The scarf that Malcolm held in his fist was draped over her shoulders. She had Charley's eyes.

Footsteps sounded in the corridor. Malcolm quickly replaced the picture, wound the box in the scarf, and placed it back into the tack box. He dropped the lid of the box closed and jumped on his bed just as Charley walked into the room.

* * *

Malcolm was reading on his bed when Charley entered.

"There you are," Malcolm said. "Been wondering. We figured you ran home, like Mullins and Bowles. Thought I might have the room to myself soon."

"Mullins?" Charley asked. He picked at a thread hanging from his pocket.

"He's run home," Malcolm said. "We've just heard."

"But he hasn't," Charley said. He tugged harder on the thread.

"What do you mean? Have you seen him? What are you on about, oik?"

"It's just that..." His face heated. *Mustn't admit where I was.*

114

What I heard... "Well, his things are still here. And I heard he was in the infirmary."

"Well, he isn't. The masters have all checked, and Byrne called his family. He's gone home."

"But his things—"

"He'll get new things, won't he?"

Charley sat on his bed. "He had no reason to leave." The pocket thread came away in his hand. "And I don't think he's home." The paper box fell onto the bedspread. It was crushed. He held it up to the light and gave it a gentle shake. Small bodies rattled at the bottom, but nothing moved. He put the box on the bedside table.

He pulled a sheet of paper and a pen from the desk in the corner.

Fairgrove Manor, York.
Mrs. Mullins,
I went to visit your son, Sean, in the infirmary at school,
but I heard he had gone home ill. I am inquiring after his health.
Please do give him my regards.
Sincerely,
Charley Winslow
Dunleigh Abbey, Old Cross School for Boys

Charley folded the note and slipped it into his pocket.

"Mister Winslow," a deep voice sounded from the doorway. It was Master Brown. "You are wanted in the headmaster's office immediately." The master turned and vanished down the hall.

Charley looked to Malcolm, who smiled, but continued to read his book.

Charley rose and walked to the door.

* * *

"You wanted to see me, sir?"

"Mister Winslow. Good to see you again. However, I understand that you have been distracting the gardener in the grounds instead of participating with the other students. It is believed that you are getting into trouble when you should be enriching yourself. Is this true?"

"I'm sorry, sir. I didn't realize I was being a nuisance to him. He was very helpful with my study of entomology and helped me locate some specimens. I'll try not to bother him again, sir." Charley felt his ears heat.

"You're here to become part of an elite society, Charley. You must involve yourself. Quit hunting the cricket and start playing it." The headmaster blew a whisky-scented guffaw.

"Yes, sir. I'll try."

"Make friends with your peers, Charley. They will be your allies throughout life."

"I'm afraid I have struggled with that a bit, headmaster. I had befriended Bowles, but...Malcolm said he's gone home." Charley locked his gaze onto the headmaster's rheumy eyes.

"Ah, Bowles. Yes. Not cut out for school life, I'm afraid. I would hate to see the same fate fall on you as has fallen on Bowles and Mullins." The headmaster stared back at Charley. "Leaving our fine school is a black mark on any record."

Charley raised his chin. The headmaster's face was dark. Charley looked at the dull shine on the brass telephone. The headmaster smirked.

Does he know? Has Sam told him of the prying into school business?

"Yes, sir," Charley said.

"Do you know why several of our dormitories are empty, Charley?"

"No, sir."

"Because the war is over. The Great War. And, all around England, families are back together. But that's not the case for many boys, is it, Charley?"

Charley swallowed. "No, sir."

"Exactly. No. Because there is always another battle, and some men are always soldiers. Their sons need homes. *This* is your home. These boys, these masters, are your family. Do you understand how fortunate you are?"

"Yes, sir." He thought of warm sand and citrus trees, music and the sea.

"I'd like to see some sign of it." The headmaster paused, stared into Charley's eyes, then nodded. "You are excused. But if I hear again that you are courting trouble, it will be another caning; do you understand?"

"Yes, sir." Charley turned to go.

As he walked back out the door, he saw the picture was back in place, its creases smoothed back behind the glass of the frame. Charley's heart sank.

He kept to the shadows on his way back to the dorms. *If you already have a home in your heart, can you make another? Even if it's lost to you?* He paused in the dark servants' staircase to breathe and collect himself before facing the other boys.

The dorm room was silent, somber. Boys sat on their beds, staring at the floor or their shoes or the walls.

When Charley entered, Malcolm stood from his bed and walked to him. His thin fingers curled over Charley's shoulders. "Charley, there's…" Malcolm's mouth moved, but no more words came.

"What is it? Is it Father?"

"I think you should go to the matron, Charley. There's news. About Bowles."

* * *

Charley made his way back through the halls, his knees nearly giving out on the steep curve of the back stairs. His breath raced and his chest began to burn. He swung himself into the infirmary and collapsed, coughing, on the floor. His vision narrowed to a small point of light. The peppermint and tea scent of Matron Grace filled his nose as he felt hands lift him and guide him to the leather chair. He let the heat from the fire soak into his cold, sweaty face.

"What's wrong with the boy? What's he doing here? I just sent him away." Headmaster Byrne's voice sounded from the mantle.

Grace's cool hand covered Charley's. "Charley, what's wrong? Can you speak?"

"Bowles." Charley forced the word into a breath as it rushed from him. He pried his eyes open. Light began to return to his vision.

The matron's hands squeezed his. "I'm so sorry, Charley. He didn't make it." The room seemed to spin like a beetle on its back. "The police were out looking for Sean, and they found Ethan. He had run out onto the moor—but he was too injured, Charley. It was too much for him."

Charley felt the tightness in his chest release all at once in a low wail. He collapsed against the matron's shoulder. "No. No, he wouldn't have left. Couldn't have run. Are they sure it was him?"

"Yes, Charley, they're quite sure. I'm so sorry."

Charley lifted his head. He looked to the headmaster, who turned away quickly. "Is he here? Can I see him?"

The headmaster made a scoffing sound and walked away. "Grace, did you send for this boy? He should be in his room with the others."

Charley glared at the headmaster's back. "He was like *family* to me."

"Charley, I'm sorry. We felt it would be best to bury him immediately. The gardener is doing it now. There will be a service tomorrow." Grace squeezed his hands again.

Sam.

"Thank you for telling me, Matron." He looked at Headmaster Byrne's frowning profile, at his crossed arms. Cold blue eyes turned to meet his. "May I be excused?"

"Of course, Charley." Grace brushed hair back from his sweaty forehead. "Go get some rest."

Charley never took his eyes from the headmaster as he walked from the infirmary and pulled the door shut behind himself. As soon as the latch clicked, the headmaster's voice rose, and the matron's came in short answer.

Charley stared across the empty entrance hall. *The headmaster lies. It might not have been Bowles. I'll see for myself. They can't stop me.* Charley walked across the hall and slipped out of the double doors and onto the grounds.

The earth around the flagstone entrance was soggy. *No tire tracks. No footprints. Were the police ever even here? Were they really even called at all? Has anyone looked for Sean?*

Somewhere, Sam was digging a grave. Charley scanned the horizon but saw no sign of the gardener. He crept along the arm of the South Wing, then around its tip. To the west, he saw Sam bent over his shovel, hauling at the cold earth. Charley kept hidden around the corner of the South Wing, peering with one eye at the man he'd thought had been his friend. He didn't dare interrupt. Didn't dare demand to look inside the long, pale wooden box at the gardener's feet.

Charley turned away. He cut across the south lawn and rounded the end of the East Wing. He ran to the muddy vegetable patch and pried a shovel from the ground. The copse of trees beyond the East Wing hid him in their shadows while he sat and waited, clawing through the pile of discarded rocks, looking for anything Bowles might have called special.

* * *

As evening fell, Charley began to shiver. *Enough. Surely Sam is finished and Bowles' long box is in the ground.* Charley climbed stiffly down from the pile of rocks, leaning on the shovel. He kept to the shadows of the trees as he circled the lawns, making his way around to the west. Sam was gone. Only a rough patch of earth marked where he had been.

Charley swept his eyes across the grounds and saw no sign of anyone. The windows of the West Wing were dark. He raced over to the patch of disturbed earth and began to dig, quickly, tossing the wet, heavy mud over his shoulder.

He reached the wood box much sooner than he thought he should. *So shallow. Not even a proper grave.*

The pale wood was smeared with mud. Charley slid the lip of the shovel under the lid of the box and leaned into it, prying, throwing his weight against the shovel. The nails squeaked as they rose from their sockets. When one end of the lid sprang loose, Charley moved to the other and wrenched at the boards. The lid came free.

Charley panted. He squeezed his eyes shut and pushed the dirty plank away from the box.

Inside, wrapped in a filthy blanket, was a pile of stones.

Crystals, shining agates, and lumpy grey rocks. *Igneous*. Charley's face heated. He dropped the shovel and ran for the school.

Why should I rebury their secrets? Let them see it. Let them all see.

He burst through the front doors and raced for the stairway, leaving slick puddles of mud behind.

He couldn't bear the thought of returning to the dorm, to Malcolm's smug taunts and the stinking piles of shoes. He didn't want to wander the grounds for exercises or military drills that only served to remind him of his father's peril, didn't want to face Sam and his betrayal. He trudged down the hall, unsure of his direction. As he turned the corner onto the South Wing second floor hall, he saw the closet door hung ajar.

He heard laughter trickling down the hallway, the sound of boys forming elite societies, carefree and careless of the lies all around them.

Charley slipped inside the closet.

There were secrets of the East Wing left unexplored, and perhaps some answers hidden there.

CHAPTER SIX

The dying light outside made no difference between the layers inside the old abbey walls, or in the tunnels below. The plank stairs and crumbling brick floors were as invisible as before. Charley could smell their age, and taste it in the dust that settled on his tongue with each breath. He trailed his hand along the wall, tracing his way, wondering if perhaps the path would split and he would discover another hidden part of the East Wing.

When he came to the second set of stairs, he climbed, and kept climbing past the glow outlining the loose board on the landing he'd used before. The stairs continued up from the landing before there was an opening. No board concealed this passage—it spilled out into an unfinished space. In all their centuries, these walls had never touched paint or plaster. They were never meant to be seen, a vestigial bowel of the old abbey. Charley stepped into the open shadows.

Dust danced in streams of light that shot through the tar-slate planks that formed a sloping roof. Rough beams spanned the space between the slopes, wide timbers hewn from ancient forests. A multitude of pale objects hung from frayed cord, dangling from the beams. Bits of old cloth, stones with holes through the centers, military medals coarse with tarnish, scissors, spools, and dried dead animals—birds and mice. The floor was rimmed with old pine crates, tack boxes—the names barely visible under layers of dust—and old chests with rusted metal braces.

The long room stretched off into a distance obscured with debris. Charley walked the length of it, dodging the hanging oddities.

A face materialized. He stifled a cry in time to notice it was a mask with black lips and hollow eyes, tattered yellow feathers trailing like hair from its edge. Charley pulled the embroidered linen scarf from under his shirt and pressed it to his lips, catching his breath in its weave.

Cold wind rushed through the spaces between the boards. *This must be the highest reach of the East Wing, the eaves above the servants' attic rooms.* Charley closed his eyes and listened to the whistle of wind, like an echo of sleeping boys in a peaceful dormitory.

Partitions carved from old beams, as thick as Charley himself, stretched out through the room at intervals, stabilizing the long roof and separating the room into alcoves filled with crates and dusty cloths draped over mounded shapes. Charley saw a glimmer of light shining through the far wall ahead. As he grew closer, he saw the walls were lined with lumpy furniture and old toys: a mangy rocking horse, a shelf of rotted picture books. A moth-eaten dress form in a child's size, still dressed in a half-finished gown. Bones dangled from the beams, knobby digits and hundreds of teeth strung on cords like pearls. A tall portrait of a young woman with dark curls lay against the wall, the canvas slashed to ribbons from her pale neck down her dark gown.

Along the other wall, under the eaves, were stacks and stacks of books. Twenty copies each of a dozen different titles, free of dust. Their embossed lettering glittered in the bars of light. Anatomy texts. Guides to the skeletal system, the brain, analysis of the chambers of the heart. The chemistry of medicine. Beside the tower of books was a pile of broken slates, each covered in scrawled anatomical illustrations. Broken nubs of chalk were scattered around them, crumbling to dust.

As he approached the final partition, he saw the corner of a dusty mattress on the floor. He stopped. Faint breathing sounded from behind the thin wall, a soft rhythm at odds with the blowing wind. He struggled to control his own rapid breath.

Charley took three quiet steps. He could see feet at the end of the mattress. They were wrapped in filthy grey rags that had been worn through to yellow, callused skin beneath, the frayed thread encased in the folded calluses, rags and flesh fused. Thick grey nails twisted from the ends of the toes. One leg lay wrenched dramatically around, withered and starved, the skin darker than its twin.

Charley froze. He wanted to see this creature's face, but fear anchored him. He forced himself forward, placing his feet at the reinforced joints of the boards to avoid the creak of old wood.

The creature came into view. The cloth around its body was disintegrating, rotting with age and wear. Pale hands lay across a sunken stomach, the fingers slender with nails so long they had begun to turn askew. Purple flesh swelled at the knuckles, where two fingers were missing.

Charley leaned, straining his neck and shoulders forward. He struggled to hold his breath as he saw the creature's face.

The face was desecrated. Breath whistled through a narrow, fleshy hole where the nose should have been. Dark, sunken skin surrounded the loose slits of his eyes. The mouth was thin and scarred—red, glossy, puckered flesh bubbling away from the opening at odd angles. Black hair tangled thinly from a speckled pate. A fine down of hair, stained with dirt, dust, and blood, covered the neck and chin. The forehead was smooth but for a jagged scar winding across its length, punctuated with a crosshatch of smaller scars. Dust coated the filthy hair, masking its dark shine in cloudy white.

Charley gazed at the disfigured boy. He couldn't be much older than twenty, but his form had aged in a century of pain. Charley's eyes burned, his throat tightening against a rising tide of pity as he inventoried the boy's many sufferings.

The boy's head stirred on the moth-eaten pillow, raising a cloud of dust and a smell of old cheese. Charley saw then that a second pillow lay alongside the first. Its linen was fresh, the faintest imprint of a head still pressed into its center.

The twisted boy stirred again, and Charley's heart leapt into his throat. He leaned back, out of sight behind the partition, and began to back away, afraid to turn his back on the poor boy. He pressed the linen scarf over his mouth and nose, the fabric growing damp with the mist of his rapid breath.

Something tapped the back of his head. Charley gasped and spun, choking as a string of dry, severed ears swung back toward his face, each ear pierced through the lobe, strung like beads onto twine.

Charley dodged the swing of the ears and paused to catch his breath. The ache of rising acid filled his throat. A gurgling snore and a moan came from behind the wall.

Charley wove through swinging bones, rushing past the collection of old toys, dolls and velvet chairs, chests and boxes. He swept aside the hanging knives and mice and plunged back into the darkness of the staircase.

The din of the evening bell sounded, shaking dust from the walls. Boys would be filling the halls of the school, returning to their rooms. He dared not walk out of the hall closet into a streaming sea of students. *I'll have to hide till the way is clear, sneak in before lights out.* He pressed through the board on the first landing he came to, the one that led into the second-floor hall.

More footprints lay scattered through the dust. Cobwebs hung in broken tatters along the walls. The doors were still all closed. Charley stepped in the footsteps to conceal his trail, following them to the dormitory door. It stood open.

Bowles' geode was back on the bedside table. Charley didn't dare touch it now.

A pile of old, bloody bandages lay next to the crystal. Charley walked to the table. His toe cracked lightly against something on the floor. A ring of marbles shone in the dust, tracing glyphic trails through the filth where they rolled.

"Oh, Sean," Charley whispered. He stepped over the ring of marbles to the table. He poked at the bandages. They were stiff at the edges, dark, and shedding dry blood in flakes like beetle's wings. But at the center they were malleable, damp with bright blood and a thin shine of pus. Fresh. A black trail of thread peeked out between the folds. Charley plucked at it. It was sturdy cotton.

Charley's heart hammered at his insides, pummeling his stomach. He dropped the thread. A pair of rusty scissors lay on the bed by the pillow. On the post of the bed hung a dirty white apron, the ties frayed, pockets stained along the bottom. Charley panted. He heard the dry metal clank of a lock and the protesting shriek of rusty hinges as a door opened in the hall.

Charley cursed. He couldn't hide here in all this dust, couldn't go unnoticed leaving a trail everywhere he walked. There was nowhere to hide. He pressed himself against the wall by the door—in the same place where, in his own room, he'd watched the twisted boy try to beat in his skull with the crystal.

He listened to many feet pad softly in the dust behind him. He heard the clink of a key and another screech of hinges, the sound of a door closing, the mechanisms sliding roughly back into place. More feet padded down the hall—a slow, quiet shuffle toward the staircase at the end.

Charley waited for the footsteps to recede and peered around the doorframe into the hall. It was empty, save for the settling cloud of stirred dust.

He dared not enter the tunnel with the East Wing astir with its secrets. He stepped into the hall and tiptoed to the servants' stairway entrance. The shuffling of feet echoed from below. He heard a scraping above and pressed himself to the side just as another quiet stream of footsteps filed past, a moaning procession down to the first floor.

Charley squeezed his eyes shut. More than a dozen boys had passed him, he was sure. Perhaps every one of the missing boys, the *runners*, was kept here, locked away by the twisted boy.

A loud clap sounded from beside him as the heavy plank to the inner-wall passage rattled to the floor. Charley's eyes shot open. He bit down on the linen scarf to stifle the rising wail in his throat as a twisted foot emerged from the dark hole in the wall.

Charley slipped into the curving servants' staircase and began to climb up to the third floor to the open windows and the only safe way out. Dry boards that had been placed over gaps in the ancient stone rattled under his feet. He plunged forward into the third-floor hall and ran, again, to the window that had saved him before.

He climbed through and lowered himself from the slab of sill, reaching his feet down, feeling for the edges of stones. The sill crumbled. He fell.

CHAPTER SEVEN

Dark, shining beads of wrapped flies studded the web like jewels hung from a fine silver chain. Light reflecting through the strands dimmed, then burst in bright spots. A soft hum sounded to his right. He tried to turn his head to look, but the bright spots grew brighter, bloomed dark, and pain grew behind them. He moaned. The humming stopped.

"Charley? Matron, he's wakin' up."

The gardener's face moved into Charley's frame of vision. Unfamiliar lines crossed his brow, like the scars on the twisted boy, but they smoothed as Charley's eyes opened more.

Charley heard the staccato of the matron's step approaching, smelled the fresh linen of her apron, the peppermint tea on her breath. "Charley, how are you feeling?" she asked, her cool hand pressing against his cheek and forehead, then his bare shoulder.

He couldn't find his voice. He chased speech through the dark tunnel of his consciousness.

The matron pressed a narrow glass bottle to his chin and a bitter, sour liquid spilled over his lip. He probed at the flow with his tongue, then drew it back, shrinking it against the roof of his mouth as the oily medicine flowed around it.

"You're going to be all right, Charley," she said as she poured.

He felt the callused hand of the gardener wrap around his forearm.

The Matron leaned over him and pried at his eyelids. The scent of medicine rising from his lips mixed with the peppermint of her breath. "You've hit your head rather badly, and I'm afraid your left arm is broken in several places. But you're lucky. Your back and legs are strained, but they'll recover."

Charley remembered the fall, then the shock of slipping, fresh every second, how soft the ground felt, how he seemed to sink into the earth, the damp woven mat of grass over spongy dirt catching him in its net. He remembered the hard arms of the gardener and the breath blowing over his face, smelling of apples.

The matron's steps receded to the far corner. The cabinet doors creaked shut.

"I told them tha fell from an apple tree," the gardener whispered in Charley's ear; the fresh apple breath had turned to hot, sour cider. "Tell them you were lookin' for bugs in th' old apples there."

Charley closed his eyes, caught his voice. "Yes." With his eyes closed, the dark washed over him. He felt a warm wet cloth and heard the slosh of water in the matron's basin. He dreamed of storm waves crashing against the rough stones of a coastal fort.

* * *

The fog lifted from Charley's eyes; the dark tunnel of his vision opened wider, let in more light, and thoughts came to him more easily. "Sam?"

"I'm here, Charley," the gardener croaked.

Charley shifted his head, found that he could turn his head somewhat, and looked to Sam. He was sitting, slouched and grim-faced, on a wooden stool.

"Thank you," Charley said.

"Ah, Charley, I wish I'd been there to catch you this time. Why were you back in that place?"

"I needed to go somewhere. To hide away. And I needed answers."

"I'll give you a key to the greenhouses, Charley. You can hide there anytime. Or a shed, if you like. But that place—that's no place to hide."

"I thought you didn't want me bothering you anymore."

"What?"

"The headmaster said you'd complained about me sneaking around the grounds and school, causing trouble. I didn't mean to be a nuisance, really. I'm sorry." Charley choked, his dry throat unable to pinch back a cough.

"I never said any such thing, Charley, not to anyone, not a soul. I'd never say that."

"But the picture I gave you—the one with your mother—I saw it back on the headmaster's wall. You didn't give it back to him?"

The gardener frowned. "The matron came to me th' other day. She said you'd been suspected in its theft and th' headmaster was demanding it be returned. She said she'd take it back and replace it for us, tell th' headmaster a student brought it to her and wished to remain anonymous. I gave it to her, and she must have done so."

"I'm sorry, Sam. I thought—"

"Never mind, Charley." The rough hand returned to his arm.

His sweat felt cold across his temples. He closed his eyes, watching his thoughts stream through the tunnel. He snatched at them randomly. "Sam," he said.

"What is it, Charley?"

"The name on the bottom of the photograph—I saw it again."

"Me mam's name?"

"Yes, I saw it on the plaque under the bust. It's the old earl. She has the same name as the earl."

The gardener rubbed his beard. "Aye, I suppose that's true, though I never knew her by that name mis'sen. She may've seen that as she came in. Given it as her name, to avoid the police on her trail."

"You said she was the daughter of a rich man."

"But the earl had no heirs. That's how this place came to be a school."

"You said she was disowned for having a child out of wedlock."

The gardener twined his fingers together. His hands were cleaner than Charley had ever seen them, scrubbed to the skin with only the faintest lines of dirt in the creases, the nails scrubbed, though stained with earth.

"Maybe when she left, after…" Charley said. "Maybe she came home."

The gardener's breathing grew ragged. He covered his eyes with his hands, then began to laugh quietly. "If tha'rt right, Charley—and I'm not saying you are—then I should be dancin' in the hall here, not pullin' nettles and diggin' rocks."

"You could have been the earl here. This would have been your house, with your face in marble on a plinth by the door."

"Black marble? Nah, Charley. This could never have been mine. Folks like me, we don't inherit big houses. No matter how much we belong to a place, it doesn't belong to us." Sam plucked at his stained nails.

"I've never belonged to a place. I don't know if I'd want to," Charley said.

"It's nice t' be home. And this is home, or summat of one. At least the grounds are, and the orchards." Sam smiled. "Aye, I don't think I'd feel so much at home in the ballroom, anyway."

Charley smiled. "I think I'd rather be digging rocks." The memory of the coffin full of rocks wilted his smile.

The gardener grinned. "A truth, Charley, a truth."

"Sam, they said you buried Bowles."

Sam dropped his gaze. "I thought I had. I might've. But the box I buried was found—dug up, full of rocks."

"You didn't see inside the box before you buried it?"

"No, no. It was sealed afore it was brought to me. I never thought…"

"Sam, I don't believe Bowles was found at all. I don't think the police were ever called. And I don't believe Bowles is dead, or Sean either."

"I don't know what to believe, Charley. I feel like I don't know owt anymore. But you'd best keep quiet. Something isn't right, and I don't know who to trust."

Charley rubbed at the sore muscles in his neck. "Where's Matron Grace?"

"She's preparin' a tray for you in the kitchens. You've been here near two days now on just tea and broth." The crease returned to the gardener's brow.

Charley shifted, testing himself. He ached all over as though he'd been shaken, each joint strained, each muscle pulled. He gasped when he tried to move his left arm. The coarse edge of plaster scraped against his skin. The two small fingers of his left hand ached, pain shooting to his shoulder. He clenched his teeth.

"Be still, Charley. The doctor from the village was here. He said your arm was shattered. Tha'll have to keep it still a long while before it heals. He wrapped it up. Said tha may have trouble with it always, that it may not ever be as it was." Sam's voice broke, choking the words out.

Charley panted through the pain. He didn't want more of the bitter oil, didn't want to be chasing his voice down that dark tunnel. He reached for Sam with his right arm and put his hand on the gardener's knee. He pushed the pain back and hummed, as his nurse had done when they'd cut away at the spider bite on his leg.

Matron Grace walked in, balancing a rattling tray on her forearm as she closed the door behind her. "Charley, you're awake!" She made no note of the gardener, but brought a rag from the cupboard.

Sam wiped Charley's face as Grace set the tray on a stand by Charley's bed. She pulled another stool from along the wall and sat. "Do you think you can lift your head, Charley, and have some porridge?"

He nodded. Even if he thought he couldn't, he felt the need to prove to Sam that he would heal. He lifted his head a bit. Sam leaned in, pressing the pillow under Charley's neck to help raise his head.

The matron began spooning porridge into his mouth. It was steaming hot and burned his tongue, but he didn't dare flinch or spit it out. Sam was sighing with relief as he watched Charley eat, and Charley was hungry enough to swallow the steaming, grainy slop. It tasted like the bottom of a dishpan, and everything seemed to have taken on the flavor of the matron's dark medicine.

The matron scraped the china bowl. The last bite was sticky and cool, but Charley's burnt tongue, rough in his mouth, barely tasted it. He swallowed and drank the cooling tea, exhausted from his brief activity.

The gardener stood. His knees cracked as he straightened them, the joints of the stool groaning in sympathy. "I'd best see t' some breakfast mis'sen, and get some work done. You rest, Charley. I'll be back this afternoon to hear how you're doin', and I'll help you write a letter t' your father. He should know you've been injured."

"Thank you, Sam. That would be nice." Charley's chest tightened at the thought of telling his father about the fall and his injuries. *Will he come? He can't. I know he can't, but…* But the dark tunnel was pulling him down, and his thoughts began to drift. When the matron pressed the bottle to his chin, he tipped his head back. The dead skin coating his burnt tongue didn't taste the bitter oil.

* * *

By evening bell, when the gardener arrived, Charley had forced himself to sit up. He'd worked at it for hours, gritting his teeth through the pain, determined to show some sign of improvement. The movement had loosened his stiff joints and stretched his cramped muscles.

His heartbeat throbbed inside the plaster around his arm. The cast ran from near his armpit, curving around his elbow, down to his wrist. It ballooned into a sphere that covered his hand. He felt his thumb pressed against his pointer and middle finger, curled in a loose fist around soft gauze that felt damp in his sweaty hand. He couldn't feel his last two fingers, except for a dull, throbbing ache that peaked at intervals.

His chest and right arm were covered in bruises. He felt tender spots on his face. The left side of his head was swollen and sore, his ear ripped and scabbed over. He could move his right leg with some stiffness, but his left knee burned and stung when he tried to bend it. It was purple and swollen, with bruises the color of soft apples. Charley breathed deeply as the magnitude of his good fortune settled on him. If he'd landed a little differently, he might have never walked again—or never breathed again, for that matter.

The gardener settled on the stool. "Tha'rt looking much better," he said, smiling.

"I'm feeling better, feeling fortunate," Charley said.

The gardener nodded. "That you are. Where's the matron?"

"I don't know. She was gone when I woke, and hasn't been back for a while." Charley looked around the room. "Is my jacket on that chair there? I had a letter in the pocket I was hoping to send as soon as possible, to Sean's parents."

The gardener crossed the room and reached a hand into each pocket. "There's nothing here, Charley."

Charley sagged. "Oh."

"Perhaps the matron sent it on already."

"Yes, I suppose she likely has," Charley said.

"I'm glad she's helped you, Charley, even if she doesn't seem t' trust me much. She's awful protective, an' I guess that's good."

"She's let you look after me here. She can't think you're too dangerous." Charley smiled, and felt the deep ache in the bruises on his face.

"That's true, and I'm grateful for it. I don't suffer worry well— rather be here t' help, though I can't do much."

"You do a lot, Sam. You're the only one that's seen me."

"Your head boy came by while you were sleepin'. Said he'd worried you'd come to trouble, but he looked relieved when I told him you'd live."

Charley raised his eyebrows. "He's probably wondering when I'll be able to polish his boots again."

Sam laughed.

Charley picked at a thread hanging from the edge of the plaster cast. "Sam, I saw the twisted boy, the one who shuffles around at night."

"A boy?" Sam asked.

"Yes—well, he's older than a student, but younger than you, I think. It's difficult to tell. He's horribly scarred. I saw him sleeping on an old mattress in the belfry attic above the East Wing. He has things there, hanging from the ceiling—ears and teeth and—" The room seemed to spin.

"Calm down, Charley." Sam stood and put a hand to Charley's chest, and one on his back, as if forcing his breath to slow. "Tha may've dreamed things, on the medicine, that are playin' as memories. They just seem real."

Charley shook his head. "No. It wasn't a dream. The attic is full of old toys and tack boxes; the ceiling is hung with bones and dry mice and things. At the end of the attic is a small room with an old mattress, and the twisted boy was sleeping there. I snuck away to the other dorm rooms. Sean's marbles were there, in a ring on the floor, just where he used to play in our room. I heard people walking around. There are more people there, I saw dirty bandages… That's when I climbed out the window."

"Perhaps tha'd better lie back, Charley, and relax a bit. You're gettin' worked up."

"Sam, I think those missing boys are all here, still in the school, locked in the East Wing."

* * *

The pain in Charley's arm woke him in the middle of the night. It jolted him, as if his fractures were live wires shaking his body with a trembling current.

He called out for the matron. There was no answer. He clenched his teeth together, sweat streaming from his brow until, like a blast of thunder, he fell back down the dark tunnel.

* * *

He woke with sunlight in his eyes. His sheets were damp, twisted around his right leg. The shadow of pain in his arm gnawed at him.

"Matron," he croaked. He heard the tap of her shoes approach.

"Yes, Charley?"

"I'm hurting more now. Rather a lot at the moment."

"Oh, Charley, I'm so sorry. I switched your medicine to one that wouldn't make you feel so sleepy. It must not be working as well for you. Would you like the old one again?"

"I think, maybe, just for a bit. I don't like the other, but..."

She hurried off and came back. Charley saw the narrow bottle in her hand. The label was green and silver, the liquid inside dark. He let it run over his tongue, not thinking about the taste or the tunnel, just the pain in his arm and fingers.

Matron Grace pulled a bloodstained strip of linen from around her throat. "Charley, when Sam brought you in, you were holding this. I'm afraid it's rather torn, but it seemed like it might be special to you. Would you like me to mend it?"

Charley fought the rising sleep. He saw the frayed silk threads of the scarf hanging from the spattered linen. His chest tightened. He wanted to reach for it, but couldn't command his arms.

"Here, Charley." She tucked the cloth against his neck, next to his face. "I'll mend it after you're asleep."

* * *

Charley opened his eyes to blackness. The night looked much like the tunnel of oblivion.

His head felt as though it tilted on a separate axis from the rest of him, spinning independently, leaving the rest of him behind. He reached his good hand to his face and touched his eyes, brushing crumbs of sleep from them, checking to see if they were truly open. They were. *Clouds must cover the moon tonight*, he thought.

He heard the stool creak to his right. *Is Sam sleeping there again? Did Matron tell him I might have trouble in the night?*

He took comfort in the coarse breathing beside him, in the fresh sheets he felt stretched over him, in the soft weave of linen by his face and the tickle of its silk threads—in the dark tunnel closing in.

* * *

In the morning, soft light filled the room. Charley pushed himself up in the bed. He turned to the stool, but it was empty. Perhaps he had dreamed the gardener there.

He stretched his muscles, flexed his stiff joints. The swelling in his left knee had gone down; the knee bent more easily, though it was still tender.

Charley pulled the sheet out from its tight tuck around the mattress and shifted his legs, swinging them around. He bent his right leg over the edge of the bed, stretching the left one out. He steadied himself with his hand on the footboard and stood, quivering. He slowly lowered his left leg, resting the sole of his foot against the floorboards, and allowed his weight to distribute in increments, testing its tolerance.

It held him fairly well, so long as his other foot bore half the burden. The pain grew too sharp when he shifted his balance. Still, it was enough for him to lean down and pull the chamber pot from beneath the bed and relieve himself.

He slowly rotated back toward the bed, leaning on it, hooking his right hand around a spindle of the headboard and pulling while pressing with his right foot, and he was back on the bed, though at a different angle than before. He faced the stool. It was dirty, covered in a fine film of dust. Trapped in one of its creaking, wobbling joints was a tangle of worn grey fibers. His heart, still racing from exertion, seemed to freeze.

"Matron!" he called. He heard a rustling behind her chamber door, the muffled steps of her feet. The door opened.

"Yes, Charley, what is it? Are you feeling all right?" He heard her walk up behind him.

"Was someone here last night?"

"Just me, Charley, and the headmaster came by to check in on you. But that's all. Why?"

"I heard someone on the stool last night, and now look." He pointed at the dust and fibers.

"It's likely plaster dust, Charley, from your cast and bandages."

"Look at these." He wriggled his arm out from under his body, twisting, and pinched the fibers. He tugged them free, leaving a few pieces stuck in the wood. He held them up to the matron. She cupped her hand and he dropped them in.

"That's what the twisted boy wears."

"Who?"

"The shuffling boy I've seen around the school—he wears rags like this. Old fibers, covered in dust. I think he was here, on this stool." Charley's voice began to shake. "Matron, will you ask Sam to come, to stay here?"

Matron sighed. "I'm afraid I can't, Charley. The headmaster brought it up—it isn't really appropriate. You shouldn't be so personal with a member of the staff. It's against the rules, and it could cost him his place. Besides, Charley—I shouldn't really discuss this with you, but there's a family history there. You'd do best to distance yourself. But you needn't worry; the headmaster has sent him to town to pick up some things, and he won't be back for a few days. I promised him I'd keep you well and have you walking by the time he's back. Don't worry over a bit of dust and rag, Charley. They're everywhere in an old school. Just the same, I'll lock the door tonight, all right?"

Charley nodded. "Matron, did you meet his mother? Sam's?"

Matron Grace looked down a moment, then looked Charley in the eye. "I replaced her. She had already been dismissed when I arrived."

"Did you know her name?"

"Eleanor Ward, I believe."

Charley swallowed, felt his throat constrict. "Just like the earl?"

"Yes, I believe there was some relation," the matron said.

"Why was she dismissed?"

"That's enough questions, Charley, and the answers aren't for children's ears."

Charley looked down at his hand, curled into a fist, knuckles white. "Matron, I don't want to take any more of that medicine—the one that makes me sleep. I think I should be fine now without it. Better, even." He kept his gaze lowered so she wouldn't see the sweat springing to his brow.

"All right, Charley." She nodded, mouth thin. "Let me go get you something to eat. You're going to need your strength to get better."

* * *

Charley leaned against the crutch under his arm. He took trembling steps forward, the matron's hands on his waist, not pressing, but there in case he should start to fall. He hadn't fallen since the previous morning. He'd jarred his cast, but seemed unharmed. The twisting pain in his arm, the ache in his fingers, remained constant. The doctor was due soon to examine him, to see if the fractures were healing. The cast would be removed and replaced. The matron had warned him that he might want more medicine again afterward. He fretted over this, fearing the pain, but fearing the dark tunnel more. He couldn't run from the twisted boy if he was unconscious. *I can't run anyway. He limps faster than me.*

He hobbled to the far end of the infirmary and back to his bed, panting from the effort, sweating from the pain.

Matron Grace brought him a basin of cool water and a cloth. He removed his shirt, finding more ease in the motions as the days passed, and wiped the sweat from his skin. His bruises were healing, fading to a yellow veined with deep purple.

He rested against the pillow, focusing on calming his fears as he waited for the doctor.

Sam would return in the morning. Charley missed him, missed his support. The matron had been kind and helpful, but distant and troubled. Charley was beginning to feel like a burden. Like he was taking too much of her time.

He drifted, watching the sun glint off the strands of web in the window.

The door creaked, and the quiet, deep voice of the doctor carried across the room. Charley's eyes grew wide. He trembled. The matron spoke softly to the doctor, and their steps grew closer, the whispers more distinct.

"Hello, Charley," the doctor said, standing over him at last. "How are you feeling today?"

"Better, I think, thank you, Doctor."

"Let's take a look, shall we?"

Charley pushed himself up with his right arm, straining until he was upright.

The doctor pulled the blanket from him, stirring a small cloud of dust that drifted on the light streaming down from the windows.

The doctor began at his ankles, pushing on joints, bending them, squeezing them, asking Charley about his pain. His knee was a bit swollen from his exercise, but less stiff and tender. The bump on his head ached from the back around through his cheekbone, but not so sharply as it had.

"You're healing well and fast, young man. Very lucky indeed. Now let's get this cast off and see. Then I'll get you cleaned up and put a fresh one on."

Matron Grace dropped a ewer that shattered at her feet. She apologized, swept the shards away with her foot, and brought Charley a cup of water. The liquid splashed over its brim as her hand shook. "Are you certain that's wise, Doctor? The injury's still so new."

"The cast is dirty, and this spot has crumbled a bit and gone soft. I'd like to take a look at how the break is sealing. We'll have a new cast on in short order. Could you begin mixing the plaster, please?"

Charley drank the water and handed Grace the cup. As she took it, she slipped the linen scarf into his hand. He felt her fingers tremble. He wrapped his fist around the scarf and took a deep breath.

The doctor took a small, serrated saw from his case and began to scratch away at the shell of plaster. Charley watched the shavings swirl to the floor. The front of the doctor's dark suit looked as if it had been powdered with snow. Occasionally he felt the cool, blunt tip of the saw brush his skin, curiously sensitive to touch after its isolation.

As the doctor rounded the curve of Charley's elbow, the matron came up behind. She held a tray with a basin of water, rags, plaster strips, and the bottle of dark oil. The silvery label reflected the darkness of the sleep inside.

The doctor's saw circled around the globe that enclosed Charley's hand. He set it aside and grasped the cast, wriggling the tips of his thumbs into the breach. He pried the sides away, plaster chipping and cracking from the bottom where it folded against itself. It came away in powdery strips, gauze shaken free of its firm enclosure.

Beneath the thickening film of plaster powder, Charley saw the skin of his arm. Purple, red, swollen. A deep, angry trench of rent muscle. The more he saw, the more the pain seemed to grow. He squeezed his eyes closed.

The doctor gasped and choked on plaster dust. Charley's eyes whipped open in time to see the doctor turn to the matron, who'd gone white, the tray rattling in her hands, water sloshing from the basin. She stared at his hand. She set the tray down and grabbed the dark bottle. She moved it toward his face as he looked down at his arm and hand.

The two smallest fingers, ringing with pain, were missing. The skin of his forearm twisted in a vortex of folded flesh, wrapped around the broken bones, which were rotated, the palm of his hand facing entirely the wrong direction.

Charley screamed and felt the cold glass of the bottle against his lips, clacking against his teeth, the bitter oil running over his tongue and down his throat, down the black tunnel. He squeezed the linen scarf. He felt the coarse stitches of the matron's sutures holding the frayed linen weave in check, trapping its silk flowers, tying them down.

CHAPTER EIGHT

Charley woke to the rattle of his own cough. His tongue burned when he ripped it away from the dry roof of his mouth. Bits of loose skin hung in strings from his gums. His head and eyes throbbed, out of rhythm with the deep, pounding ache in his arm. He struggled to peel his eyelids back. A sticky glue coated his lashes. He raised his right hand and wiped at them, brushing away the goo and gritty crumbs.

The spider's web had grown, spanning the window many times over, stretching to the ceiling, where tattered older strands hung like curtains beaded with the dry bodies of flies. The air was smoky and dark; clouds of dust drifted in front of the cobweb-curtained windows.

Charley shivered and reached for the blanket. A piece of it came away in his hand, crumbling fibers turning to dust between his fingers.

Sleepy confusion weighed down his thoughts, pushing them

back toward the darkness. He struggled against sleep, forcing his eyes wider. He shook his head, and dust rose around him. Moths took flight from his pillow. *Hofmannophila pseudospretella*, brown house moths, flapping erratically through the murky sunbeams to the upper reaches of the room, where they became snared in hanging tendrils of web.

Charley looked down to his toes. His stocking feet stuck out from a pile of old rags, brushing the flaking enamel from the footboard, the steel beneath it the color of rust and old blood.

He pushed himself into a sitting position, the palm of his hand digging into twisted springs in the thin mattress.

Bent beds lined the long walls, piled high with old rags. Shards of broken bowls and pitchers cluttered the tops of bedside tables. The basin at his side was full of dark water, a brown moth floating on its foamy surface. A bloody rag hung over the side. Beside it stood the bottle with the silver label, only a small line of dark oil left at its base.

Charley's rapid breath echoed through the room, a dark twin to the matron's bright infirmary. He slid himself to the edge of the bed and swung his legs down. His knees trembled, but they held him. He gripped the footboard with his right hand, pressing his left arm to his chest. A hard new cast enclosed it; the white plaster had already gathered dirt and dust. He shuffled his foot, hopping and sliding, putting as little weight on his left leg as possible. Dirt and debris ploughed up between his toes. He kicked bits of splintered wood and fractured china aside, shuffling around a dry, furry mound.

He limped, footboard to footboard, down the length of the room, leaning across the narrow expanses between the beds. The front of the room had a large old leather chair: the leather dry and cracked, filthy cotton and wool spilling from the fissures. A desk perched in the corner next to a tall cabinet, the wood of both warped and splintered. The cabinet doors hung at odd angles, revealing shelves filled with dull glass bottles stopped with mildewed corks and filled with dark liquids. A pile of empty green medicine bottles sat mounded in the corner, spilling out across the floorboards that were coated in mold like black powder.

He hobbled to the door at his right, eyes cast behind him at the door that would have led to the matron's chamber.

The double doors were more ornate than those in the real infirmary. Carved roses climbed up the length of wood. Scratches ruined its surface in parallel tracks, like claw marks. Charley pulled at the lever. He tugged, but the heavy doors held fast. Through the keyhole, he could see only darkness.

He turned and slid his way back to the narrow door beside the mantle, placed his hand on the round knob, and turned. The tarnished brass felt cold and gritty, sticking to his hand like nettle. He felt the lock catch. He pulled. The door rattled in the frame, but stuck firm.

Charley turned and scanned the walls. No other doors; just long expanses of stone and wood panel, the windows high-set and firmly boarded over.

Charley's throat tightened. His heart raced, and breath burst from his mouth in rapid puffs that hung in the cold air.

He searched for something he could use to pick the locks, to break a door, or to climb to a window. The pain in his arm peaked. He whimpered and sank to the floor, too tired to crawl to a bed, in too much pain to struggle against the doors. He lay on the floor and shook. The black tunnel pulled him under.

* * *

Pain woke him. It couldn't have been a long time later; faint light still crept through the cracks between the boards on the high windows.

A stinging ache raced up his arm from his missing fingers. It wrapped around his twisted bones and up his shoulder. Charley cried out before he could stop himself.

He focused on breathing, on calming and controlling his pain. His eyes darted to the shallow line of medicine in the dark bottle, but he fought the urge, needing his mind clear, needing to be ready to face the danger, the creature—the boy—that had trapped him here.

He pushed himself off the floor and climbed onto a bed. He choked on the dust that drifted up around his face. The rusty metal joints shrieked under his weight.

The best he could do was think, and plan.

By the height of the ceiling and the carved double doors, and the exactness of the copy of the real infirmary, Charley guessed he was on the first floor, near the bricked-over juncture of the abandoned wing to the main hall. Behind the small door would be a living quarters. Above him, two floors of dark, twisted dormitories, classes, and studies. Then the staff attic with its boiling pot of offal soup. Then the long, dark chamber of the twisted boy, just below the roof.

He knew at least a dozen people walked these halls: the twisted boy, and the quiet walkers kept locked in rooms along the upper floors. He knew that the second floor and the eaves had access to the tunnel weaving through the walls and under the school, up to the second-floor closet in the South Wing.

Charley searched the room with fresh eyes, looking for a space that might conceal an opening. He stood, renewed by rest and hope. It seemed every chamber here had a secret. He just had to find the one for this room.

He explored behind each table, under each bed, working his way up the room. He looked beneath the chair, in the fireplace, behind the desk. He pulled the bottles from the cabinet, prying them out of dry, sticky puddles, and pressed against the backboards, sliding his hand along the wall behind it.

His cage was complete. He supposed this creature of the underground byways wouldn't have locked him in a room so easily bested.

Exhausted again, he dropped into the old leather chair. Had he not been so tired, the smell might have prompted him to move. Instead, he slept.

The low, slow groan of old metal awakened him. His sticky eyes pried open. He watched the long lever of the main door rotate, pointing down; then the heavy, crooked mass of door moved into the room.

CHAPTER NINE

From behind the door came the half-dragged step of the twisted boy. He halted his way past Charley before he started, noticing him in the chair. The boy carried a broken plate, which he placed on the small table by Charley.

Charley, numb with fear, stared at him. At his tangled black hair, powdered grey with dust. At his hands, missing fingers, and his twisted leg.

Charley's eyes widened and rose to the boy's, peering into the dark, rapidly darting irises. "Help me, please," he whispered.

The boy's gaze froze and focused on Charley's, the pupils shrinking back from the irises like stones falling in a well. He began to mutter and whisper, his remaining fingers coming together in a writhing tangle. "This is our school this is our school this is *our* school..."

"Please," Charley said. He reached for the boy's hands. "Just let me go."

The boy lashed out. He raked his curving nails across Charley's face, leaving three tracks of fire. Charley screamed.

The boy backed from the room, stumbling over his foot. He scrambled through the door and pulled it shut before Charley could limp after him. The key jabbed into the lock and the gears ground into place.

Charley roared and pounded at the door. He hollered till his voice broke. He stood, shaking, and pressed his forehead to the carved wood. Blood dripped from his face. He put his hand to his cheek and felt the cuts there, jagged rips burning in the salt of his sweat. He felt the tickle of blood running under his collar and reached to pull his shirt loose. His fingers found the smooth weave of the linen scarf, wrapped tightly around his throat. It soaked up the blood running from his face. He rubbed the fabric between his fingers, felt the smooth silk flowers, the rough suture stitches put there by the matron. The scarf didn't smell like his mother anymore, but like the bitter tang of medicine, sour blood, and dust.

He stumbled back to the chair. The plate caught his eye. Atop it was an assortment of table leavings—half-eaten discarded scraps from the plates of the proper school, a crust of bread and chicken skin, dry and curling at the edges. The crust was bent in half, the soft center chewed out, leaving the stiff edge behind.

He didn't know how long he'd been here, or how long he would yet be here. He reached for the rancid food and saw a small fly crawl across it. He lowered his fingertip into the fly's path and let it crawl across his hand. *Fly free, little one.* He blew gently, and the fly took off, disappearing into the shadows above.

Charley rolled the cold chicken in the dry bread and stuffed it in his mouth, holding his breath against the sweet smell of rot. The wounds in his cheek burned as he chewed. He choked it down.

He shivered, and sweat ran into his eyes. His arm itched fiercely under his cast. When he closed his eyes the room spun, draining him, pulling him under. Each time he blinked, it was more difficult to pull his eyes open again, until he didn't.

* * *

A loud bang above his head jarred him awake. He twitched, jumping, and his sore joints screamed, his arm shocking him with pain. The clatter above continued.

Charley opened his eyes as wide as they would go, soaking up the faintest glow of stars filtering through the boarded windows.

Heavy footfalls thundered across the ceiling. They pounded overhead, and another loud bang echoed through the quiet wing. Muffled cries filtered down through layers of wood and stone. Charley gripped the armrest of the old leather chair, pressing the bulb of his cast to his lips. He tasted plaster and the East Wing floor.

A clink of metal sounded next to him, the squeak of a small lock, and Charley felt the breeze of someone moving swiftly by. He felt cobwebs brush his cheek as the figure rushed from the small chamber to the locked main door. He heard the lock groan, the gears disengage, and the figure flew out the door, slamming it and locking it behind. He caught the faint scent of sour medicine on the draft in the figure's wake. Charley's fingernails splintered against the arm of the chair, his heartbeat thundering, blending with the pounding still coming from above.

Charley caught his breath. His heart skipped. He hadn't heard the small chamber door close.

He stood and walked around the chair, praying he'd find the door open. Hand outstretched, he pushed the panel of dry wood. It gave against his touch.

A faint smell of smoke drifted through the dark room. He turned to his right and followed the crumbling wall. He passed a broken chair. His fingers brushed dry moths from a tattered wall hanging. When he turned the corner, his toe knocked into a small table. A warm candle was stuck to the wood with melted wax. Charley's fingers scrambled over the table, searching, until he found a match. The dirty room blazed into view.

The pounding overhead stopped in one final, violent crash.

Debris covered the floor: crumbling stone and broken wood, shattered glass and china. Spilled bottles of medicine littered a table on the far wall, their sticky residues blending in oily puddles that soaked into the wood. A thin patchwork curtain hung from a wooden beam emerging from the stone wall.

Charley edged closer, extending the candle's light. He saw the scuffed toes of shoes under the ratty hem of the curtain, but heard no sound, saw no movement. When he crossed the room, he saw the curtain was stained with blood and covered with pockets at odd angles, pieced together from old aprons like the one the matron wore. And the matron before her.

The grind of the lock sounded from the infirmary entrance. Charley lunged across the room. He grabbed the matches and blew out the candle, hobbling through the chamber door, pulling it closed behind him as the lever of the main door handle began to rotate.

Charley shoved the candle into his tucked shirt, the hot wax burning his skin as he limped, hopping through the debris as far into the room as he could get as the door swung open. He dove behind a bed, pressing his cheek to the dirty floor.

Light footsteps tapped across the room, pausing at the chamber door. He heard the key in the lock and prayed the person wouldn't notice the lack of resistance in the mechanism. He saw a flash of white as the figure swirled into the dark room.

Charley pushed himself up and hobbled to the bed closest to the main door. He slid underneath it just as the chamber door banged back open. A low growl echoed from the doorway, and steps advanced down the center of the room, between the rows of beds. He heard the sharp retort of something crashing against each bed, heard the figure choke on the cloud of dust rising from the impacts. Charley pressed his face against his shoulder, breathing through the fabric of his scarf to filter out the filth stirred into the air.

He flinched when the bed above him rattled. The figure hollered, the scream rising an octave: a woman's voice. She stalked back into the chamber. Charley heard the clatter of wood and the shattering of glass, then silence.

He stayed under the bed, waiting, listening. There was no sound. He shook in the dust under the bed, afraid to expose himself, afraid that the woman in white waited for him.

He grasped a broken shard of china from the floor and slid out from under the bed, steadying himself, facing the dark room.

Nothing came at him except the faint flutter of moth wings. He stepped forward. The pain in his knee paled, fading with the adrenaline coursing through him. He grasped the china in his teeth and reached into his shirt, pulled out the candle and matches, and lit the wick. He walked toward the chamber.

The key had been left in the door lock.

He stuck the candle to the desk and pulled the key from the lock, tucking it into his shirt with the matches. He grabbed the candle, spilling hot wax across his fingers, and walked farther into the room. A large wood panel lay in the center of the room, pulled away from an entrance to a dark pit in the floor.

Charley backed away, through the door. More chambers and tunnels. More secrets.

He stepped back into a warm body. Hands came up and grasped his shoulders.

CHAPTER TEN

Charley choked on the scream rising in his throat, and a rough hand clamped over his mouth. He smelled copper and dirt, tasted the sticky film of blood.

He twisted in the firm grip. A rough face came down to his, brushing against his cheek, making the jagged cuts there sing with pain.

"Hush, Charley." The scent of apples.

Charley stilled, silenced, breathing heavily, sucking in the dust and dirt, the blood and apples.

The hand came away from his mouth. The other rough hand took the candle from him.

"Charley, are you all right?" The gardener's face, lit from below by the dim flame, looked dark and strange. Blood ran from his nose into his thick beard. One eye swelled, the slightest glint of white shining through the thick purple lids.

"Sam, what are you doing here? How did you get in?"

"I came t' help you."

"How did you know I was here? How did you find me?"

Sam stepped back. His face grew grim as the shadows crept across his bruises. "Th' headmaster said you'd run home. But I saw your injuries, Charley—I knew tha couldn't have run. Certainly not t' Cairo."

"Why did you leave me? Why did you go to the village when I was still sick?" Charley's strength broke. He sank to the floor, all the rage and fear pouring out of him.

"I'm sorry, Charley." Sam knelt by him. "Th' headmaster ordered me t' go. He said the matron was concerned about me—about my past, and our friendship—how much tha seemed to rely on me, and not on the school, as your family. He said a few days away would do you wonders. He said he needed me t' fetch some things." He reached out and smoothed Charley's hair, pulling bits of old rag from its tangles. "I was wrong t' go. I should have stayed."

Charley's chest tightened. He wanted to yell, but he wanted friendship more.

"When I was in town, I asked questions. About what you told me."

Charley lifted his head. His strained face had pulled at the cuts on his cheek, which flowed afresh.

"You were right, Charley. Me mam was the daughter of the earl. This was her home. And she was disowned because of a child, Charley—but that child wasn't me."

"What?" Charley straightened.

"She had a daughter, long before she met my father. The little girl went missin', and the earl disowned my mother when she wasn't found. He accused her; that's when she ran away with my father."

"But did they know it was her when she came back here to work?"

"Aye, they did. The headmaster's a friend of the late earl. He knew my mother—knew her as a child, and hired her on as matron. The woman I spoke to, she said there were rumors about a falling out between the earl and Byrne around the time my mother ran away. It was rumored that maybe Byrne had been the father of the missing girl. The earl demanded that Byrne's home be searched. Nothing was found. And Byrne refused his friendship after, though he was left the mastery of the school in the earl's estate." Sam pulled an apple from his pocket and handed it to Charley.

"Sam, there was a woman here just a moment ago. She was in that room, and she went through the hole in the floor." He shook, clutching the apple.

Sam grasped the shard of china that had fallen at Charley's feet. The light from the candle wavered across the walls as it trembled in Sam's hand. He stepped into the room. There was a low cry, and the light dropped and winked out as the candle hit the floor with a soft splash of wax.

"Sam!" Charley heaved himself off the floor and ran to the doorway. He heard the apple roll into the dark hole.

"Stay back, Charley. I'm fine. She—she's here."

"She is?" Charley's face went cold with fear.

"Yes. My mother. She's been here all along." Sam's voice was as cold and rough as stone.

Charley reached into his shirt and pulled out the matches. He groped on the floor for the candle, and lit it.

Behind the patched curtain, the corpse of an old woman sat in a splintered chair. Her skin had shrunk to leather, her hair a web of dust, wisps blending with the cobwebs stretching around her. A folded linen cap lay in her lap, yellowed, pressed between her gnarled hands, resting on a crisp, ancient apron.

Sam's shoulders shook. Charley pulled at his arm. Sam rose, and Charley led him to the leather chair. He took the callused hand in his.

"We have to leave. There's someone else here. The woman—the one who was here before—she went into that tunnel thinking she was chasing me. I don't know how long we have before she realizes I'm still in this room."

Sam swallowed and nodded.

Charley stood and walked to the main door. It gaped, ajar, another key sticking from the lock. Charley pulled the key free and placed it in his shirt with the other. He grasped the gardener's hand and pulled at him. "Come, now. We have to get out of here."

Sam stood and followed Charley, his open eye roving, searching the floor for answers.

They entered the hall outside the dark infirmary. Charley locked the tall door behind them.

The wall of flaking red brick cut off what had been the way to the main hall.

"How did you get here?" Charley asked.

Sam led him down the long hall, past walls covered in moth-eaten tapestries. He pulled one aside and slid a board from the wall. "I couldn't find the tunnel, Charley. So I took a page from your book, and climbed up through th' window you fell from." He handed Charley the candle, and they stepped through the opening. Sam pulled the board back into place behind them.

"I was searchin' the rooms for you. The boy was there in an open room. The twisted boy who chased you. We fought. I took his key." Sam swatted at cobwebs and helped Charley over the uneven floor. "I tried all th' other doors on that floor, but they were locked. I heard footsteps on the stairs, so I followed. I didn't see owt else, but I found a hole in th' wall that led me here, and this door fit the key."

The tunnel became stairs. Charley leaned on Sam as they climbed. "He'll be waiting for us up there? The twisted boy?" He hesitated on a step, resting his knee.

Sam faltered. "He's dead, Charley."

Charley felt his face burn as it twisted with grief and relief.

"I hit him, and—there wasn't much to him. Poor boy."

Charley followed Sam's footsteps in silence.

"I think tha's right about another thing, Charley."

Charley waited.

"When I was tryin' all the doors, thinkin' you were behind one of them, I heard things. I think there are more boys here, locked in like you were."

"I know there are; I've seen them. They're hurt, and drugged." *All those empty bottles of medicine…they must think they're in a bad dream.* Charley grabbed Sam's arm. "Sam, we have to get them out. Bowles might still be here, and Mullins."

"They were hurt afore they disappeared, weren't they? Like you."

"Bowles was hurt. Sean felt sick…"

"The woman in the village said that boys have gone missin' from this school since it began—always boys who had been ill or injured. My mother—" Sam paused and caught his breath. "There was an investigation. They blamed her. It was said she performed unnecessary surgeries. Some boys died. Some just vanished. That's why she was dismissed, Charley."

Charley panted, struggling to keep up on the long stairs. He stopped and lowered himself to a step to catch his breath.

Sam stopped and turned back to him, bringing the candle up between them. He reached out and wiped away the sweat and blood that ran down Charley's face.

"Sam, it never stopped."

"What didn't?"

"The surgeries."

"What?"

"When the doctor came to remove my cast, I remember the look on his face just before I passed out. My arm's twisted around. Two of my fingers are missing. Just like that poor boy."

Charley felt heat rise up in his face. He leaned over a stair and vomited, the recollection of his twisted skin turning his stomach. He felt the dry pieces of the table scraps scratch at his throat. His back slid lower against the wall.

Sam held on to him. His hands shook as hard as Charley's. "But my mam—that must have been her. I mean, I couldn't really tell, but her cap and apron…"

"Help me up, Sam. We have to keep moving. We have to get the others out." Charley's fingers pulled at the gardener's sleeve.

Sam lifted Charley and set him on his feet, holding him steady till his stance was sure. He let Charley walk ahead, keeping a hand to his back, walking close behind him in case he fell.

At the top of the long stairs, they pulled aside the loose plank and stepped into the second-floor hall. Sam paused and listened. They crept down the hall to an open doorway, stepped inside, and shut the door behind them.

A dirty bed, a reeking chamber pot, and a stack of broken, dirty plates filled the room. The smell was enough to weaken Charley's knees.

The twisted boy lay on the floor, his eyes staring, as dull as the dusty windows. His high cheekbone was caved in on the side of his face where Sam must have struck him. Charley knelt by him. The three remaining fingers on his right hand still had Charley's blood under their splintered nails. His face was smooth in death, its grimace cleared, and Charley saw, again, how young he must be. Maybe eighteen. The grey in his hair was all dust and crumbled plaster. The ankle of his twisted foot was red and withered, like Charley's arm.

"He must have been one of the missing boys," Charley said, moving a lock of hair away from the dark, empty eyes. "One of the first—mad with pain and drugs and loneliness. How long have they all called him a ghost? Never coming to look for him." He pressed the boy's eyelids shut.

Sam looked down at the boy, at Charley. He rubbed the scar on his neck. "Come, Charley. I don't think we have long before we're noticed."

Charley stood. He covered the twisted boy with a ratty blanket.

In the hallway, Charley pulled both keys from his shirt. He tried each one in every door along the long hall. Nothing moved. Charley slammed his hand against the door. "There have to be more keys."

Something slammed into the other side of the door.

Charley fell back, then pressed his face back against the wood panels. "Hello? Who's there? This is Charley! I'm going to get you out!"

Low growls slipped through the keyhole and around the door. Slow scratching slid down the dry wood. Thumps, bangs, and low moans.

"I don't think we should open this one, Charley. We shouldn't assume we have friends behind these doors."

Charley stared at the rattling wood. "I don't care if they're friends or not. Pain has made these boys monsters. We can help them."

"Charley, tha can't save what isn't there anymore."

"Bowles? Mullins?" Charley shouted through the keyhole. He heard the groan of bedsprings and something heavy hitting the floor, dragging. The bloody, scarred stumps of truncated fingers pushed under the door.

Charley coughed and raced down the hall, trying the keys again, pounding, rattling the doorknobs. "Let's go back and search the boy. There are more keys here somewhere."

"I searched him, Charley. Th' only key he had on him was t' your door."

Charley held the keys to his forehead, pacing. "The boy lived under the roof, up in the attic eaves, in that room full of boxes and hanging things. The bones…"

Charley turned and limped into the hall. The panel lay on the floor, the entrance to the tunnel gaping. Charley couldn't remember if they'd replaced it. He hobbled down the hallway.

A moan sounded to his left. He turned. The door to the dorm room was ajar. Charley looked at Sam. "This was locked, wasn't it? Before?"

Sam shook his head and shrugged. Charley pushed the door open.

Bowles lay on the bed. His crystal sat beside him on the sloping table. Charley ran to him. "Bowles! It's Charley. Are you all right? Ethan?"

Sam walked up to the other side of the bed. He looked from Bowles to Charley, his brow furrowed.

Charley reached for Bowles. At first, he thought his head had been shaved—the spiked thatch of blond hair only showed in random patches. But as the light from the candle fell over him, Charley saw white bone, and the dry yellow edges of Bowles' scalp peeling away from his skull. Rows of slanted stitches held the rest in place, infection bubbling up from the wound like tallow.

Charley swallowed his scream, breathing shallowly, the sweet scent of rot heavy on the air. "Ethan, can you hear me?"

Bowles' eyelids fluttered but didn't open.

Charley knelt low to whisper, but saw Bowles' ears were gone, cut away from angry, gaping holes. He grasped Bowles' hand. It was dry and hot, limp and unmoving.

"You can't help him, Charley."

A wail snuck past Charley's throat.

Sam came around the bed and lifted Charley away.

"I should have come straight here, Sam. I should have been sooner—I would have been in time."

"Quiet, Charley. Time forgot about this place long ago." He carried Charley from the room and into the hall, to the entrance of the tunnel. He set him down on the landing. "Up or down, Charley? It's up to you. I'll follow, and help, either way."

CHAPTER ELEVEN

"**D**o you think we can help any of them, Sam? Is it too late?"

"I don't know, Charley." Sam brushed dusty, blood-flecked black curls back from his bruised forehead.

Charley stared down the stairs into the black tunnel that led to class bells and shoe polish and ink. He climbed the stairs toward old bones.

They stepped into the long attic room. Sam cupped his hand around the candle, shading it from the swinging things that hung from the ceiling beams. They advanced past stacks of boxes, past the rotten furniture and peeling old toys. The candlelight pushed back the shadows, more than the anemic light had done the last time Charley was here. He could see wooden horses ridden by tin knights, and row upon row of linen-bodied dolls with glass faces and tattered hair. The paint of their faces had faded, coral lips worn to white.

Wind blew through the cracks between the roof slats, knocking the dangling horrors into each other, and into their shoulders as they wove a path toward the last partition. Bones on strings rang like chimes.

Charley stepped around the wall into the small sleeping space. Sam walked up to the low table and lit the other candles there. The dark receded across the dirty mattress, the small child-sized furniture, and a long low shelf along the sloping wall.

The shelf was covered in saws, syringes with long lead needles, and dusty spools of thick black thread. Beneath the shelf was a row of shoes, from tiny satin slippers to petite brown boots to shining black ones set up on dainty heels. Above the shelf hung a row of aprons, grey and bloodstained, a gradient of varied carnage, till the one that hung on the right, white and crisp and clean. It glowed in the candlelight. From its hook hung a ring of keys.

Charley grabbed the keys, stumbling over the edge of the reeking mattress. Sam pulled him back by the collar of his shirt and steadied him. Charley handed Sam the keys, and he put them in his jacket pocket as they each grabbed a candle from the table.

"These must have been my mother's toys," Sam said, as they passed a velveteen bear spilling sawdust from its neck.

"Maybe they belonged to the little girl who disappeared."

Sam's eyes widened, reflecting the flames from the candles. He looked around at the toys: at dolls arranged in circles around tiny tea sets, at empty medicine bottles next to sticky teapots. Birds hung by their feet from the rafters in cages constructed of splintered wood tied together with bits of twine.

Sam pulled at his beard. Dry blood rained from it in flakes. "Charley, I don't think the earl looked very hard for his missing granddaughter."

"What do you mean?" Charley stopped and turned to the gardener, to the row of broken teacups hanging from wooden slats.

"I don't think she was missing. I think she was hidden here, under his roof, the whole time. Just like the boys."

"You think he hid her here?"

"I think my mother did. Look at all this, Charley. I think she hid her baby here and told th' earl she'd gone missing. Maybe she hoped he'd forgive her shame. Forget her sin, if it wasn't walking 'round th' house."

"But he disowned her instead, and she ran away."

Sam picked up a small porcelain doll. "Can you imagine growin' up here? Alone in an attic. That poor child. Someone bought these toys, though, later. These aren't a baby's things. Someone knew she was here and took care of her. Sort of." He pulled a long needle from the doll's back.

"Headmaster Byrne," Charley said.

Sam dropped the doll. It shattered, sparkling pieces scattering in the candlelight. "We have to get out of here, Charley, now, away from this school. If he's behind all this, and finds out that we know—"

They turned and rushed for the stairs, swatting the hanging horrors from their faces.

At the landing, Charley leaned into the hall. "Come quick—just for a moment."

"Charley—"

Charley ran, and darted into the dorm room. Bowles still lay on the bed. Charley walked up to him, Sam following close behind. "I'm sorry, Ethan. I'll send help, I promise."

A bell rang far above them: the matins. Morning had come.

Sam poked his head into the hallway and hollered. He jumped back into the room. "Charley, *now*."

"What's wrong?" Charley paled.

"The doors are opening. All of them."

Charley reached down and squeezed Bowles' hand. His fluttering eyelids had stilled and slid back from the yellowed sclera. The ragged fever breathing had ceased. "He's gone," Charley said. "We were too late."

"We're going to be too late if we don't leave now, Charley."

"We could lock the door here, and break through the window."

"You can't climb now, and I've nothing to lower tha with. It's the tunnel or nowt, Charley."

They ran into the hallway. The heavy doors were swinging open. Swaying shadows stretched across the floor as a cloud of dust rose from shuffling footsteps.

They climbed through the tunnel entrance and fit the board back into place. Sam leaned against it, listening. Something thudded against the wood. "Go, Charley!"

Charley's knee stung as he forced it to bear the weight of his forward descent. "I'm down," he called back up the stairs. He could see the faint glow from Sam's candle, and heard the board clatter to the floor as Sam left it and raced after.

"Keep running, Charley!"

They plunged into the clay brick walkway. The tunnel was empty as far as the candlelight shone, reflecting off the slick mud on the damp walls. They raced over the crumbling brick and climbed the next set of stairs, up inside the walls of the South Wing at last, away from the ruin and rot.

No sound of footsteps chased them. They reached the top landing. Charley threw himself against the board panel. It held. He kicked at it. The board thudded, unmoving.

"Charley?"

"The door was here. This is the back of the closet by my dorm. It's supposed to open." Charley's eyes flashed white with panic. "We've been sealed in."

Sam let out a long breath that guttered his candle flame. "We have to go back to get out."

Charley sank to the floor and sat against the side wall. The boards at his back shifted just enough to make him flinch. His heart leapt. "Sam, try this one. Something moved."

Charley stood, and Sam pushed at the side boards. The wood groaned and squeaked, but it moved. Sam leaned into it, bracing his foot against the gritty floor, and heaved. The boards fell away. The stairs continued up.

CHAPTER TWELVE

"**D**oes tha know where that goes, Charley?"
Charley shook his head. "I didn't even know it was there. But if it's like the East Wing stairs, it goes to the attic."

"Well, it looks like our only way. Let's count on them not knowin', either, or them believin' you don't know."

They climbed through the opening. Sam lifted the heavy plank and pushed it back into place, forcing it flush with the surrounding walls.

The stairs were narrower than the ones below, steeper and dustier. Sam's foot snapped through one of the steps, splitting the dry plank. "Stay at the edges, Charley, over the stones. Step lightly."

They moved more slowly then, stepping where the wood met the rock and beams that laced the walls. At the top of the stairs was a narrow landing, open on one side to another long attic room. On the other side, a spindle ladder reached up to an access panel in the roof.

They crossed into the long sub-roof attic. It stretched off into the darkness, a maze of old crates. They wove through the stacks of boxes till they reached the back wall. It was deserted—just dusty storage, no hidden beds or hanging bones. The only footprints in the dust were their own.

"We must be above the South Wing. Do you think they'll follow us here?" Charley sat on a crate, rubbing at his sore legs with his hand.

"I don't know, Charley. I don't even know if they know this is here." Sam searched around the crates behind the back partition. "Charley! Look." Behind a large crate, a folding ladder sat atop a hinged door in the floor. "That must lead to the servants' quarters in th' attic of the South Wing. These must be their things stored here." Sam pulled at a segment of the ladder. Its hinges squeaked. "I doubt th' others—from the East Wing—would risk comin' here."

"Should we go down?"

Sam lay the ladder back down. "I don't think so. Not now. If Byrne is behind all this, some of the staff might be, as well. If we came crawlin' out of their attic—a missing boy, and the old matron's son…"

"Then what do we do?"

Sam looked at Charley. Charley's face was coated in blood that still oozed from the cuts on his cheek. Sweat dripped in his eyes, though he sat shivering on the crate. His cast was black with filth. "Rest, Charley. We'll make a spot for tha t' hide here in the crates. I'll keep an eye out for trouble. It's midmorning now; when it gets dark again, when all the servants are in bed, we'll sneak down. We'll get out of the school and head for the village. Go to the police."

"Sam, I saw the police in town. They love the headmaster. They'd been friends as kids."

"It's our only chance, Charley. We have proof here. An' the village knows—has always known—summat wasn't right here. They'll stand behind us, Charley. They've probably been too afraid t' speak out. Too many of them work here, or have family that do. It's easier to look away, Charley, if you're not sure of a thing. But if we show them, they'll stand up."

Charley nodded. He felt his muscles start to melt the moment he thought of rest.

Sam shifted some crates, careful not to disturb the dust around them, and lifted Charley into a hidden opening in the stack. "Lie down. I'll stay here where I can see the door."

"Thank you, Sam."

Sam nodded. "Thank you, Charley, for trusting me, even though…"

Charley smiled. "Matron Grace told me not to. She knew some of your story. About what your mother did to the students. She didn't tell me—said it wasn't for children's ears—but I can tell, now, that she knew."

"Aye, Charley, I think she knows too much."

"What do you mean?"

"My mother's dead, Charley. That was her corpse in that chair, I'm certain of it. So who's been takin' the boys? Who's been buildin' this school of monsters?"

"Byrne, I thought. And the twisted boy. And the daughter? You think she's still here?"

"That must be the woman you saw, Charley. She must have learned from *our* mother."

"And you think she's…"

"All of the missing boys vanished from th' infirmary, Charley."

Charley shook his head, hooked his fingers into the scarf. "She took care of me, though, when I was hurt. And she helped Bowles."

Sam sighed. "Charley, I believe she drugged you and tortured your arm. I believe she and that twisted young man of hers have been carrying injured boys from th' infirmary into those rooms and disfigurin' them. Drugging them till there's nowt left of the lads. If she grew up locked away, hidden in that attic…it must have been lonely, Charley. Maybe she envied the students. Maybe she wanted to be a part of the school. Maybe she took the things she wanted and made her'sen a home. Stole her friends, tried to make a family. What wouldn't tha do, if that was all tha'd known?"

Charley shook his head again. His eyes burned. He tried to think of life without his father, his nurse. Of never having had those years with his mother, few and sweet. Charley had had everything, but no home to put it in. This girl had had a home, but nothing in it.

Neither worked well without the other.

"Charley, I want to be wrong. But if you see Matron Grace, run. Just run. We'll sort it all out with the police later, but for now, don't take chances."

Charley dropped his head back into the shadows of his hidden alcove. He nodded. He didn't trust himself to speak, felt his voice trapped in his throat.

"Thank you, Charley. Now rest. It'll be dark again in five or six hours."

Charley lay down on the rough floor. He rested his head on his good arm and held his injured arm to his chest. The cast was sticky with blood, coated in dust and dirt. He closed his eyes and saw the smooth brow of the twisted boy. He squeezed his eyes shut tighter and saw the ivory curve of Bowles' skull, the shrunken leather of the dead woman's face. He whimpered, and breathed, and hummed his spider's song, picturing the long, shining filaments in the window before this nightmare started.

* * *

Charley woke to a soft hand on his mouth. His eyes flew open, and he looked into the pale face of Matron Grace. His chest tightened, his rapid breath fighting against her knuckles.

"Shh, Charley, it's all right. You're safe now. I'm here." She took her hand from his mouth and brushed the hair back from his forehead. She slipped her hand behind his neck and helped him sit up. "How are you feeling, Charley? What happened to your face? Are you hurt? I brought your medicine."

Charley stared at her. In her hand was a green bottle, its cracked label stained in the shape of a seven-legged spider. He was cornered in his ring of crates. "Where's Sam?"

"It's all right, Charley. You're safe now."

"How did you find me?"

"A maid heard voices above her room. Everyone's been looking for you and Sam. I came up the ladder."

"What happened to Sam?"

"Don't worry about him. You're safe now."

Charley struggled to his feet. His joints felt frozen after his rest, like they'd locked themselves against any further strain.

"Charley, don't—"

He pushed past her into the long room.

Sam lay sprawled on the floor, a small pool of blood by his head. A loose plank from a crate lay across his chest.

Charley rushed for him. Matron Grace caught his arm. "What happened? Is he okay?"

"Charley, stay back. He's dangerous. The headmaster believes he's responsible for the disappearance of the boys." She pulled Charley close. "God, I thought you were one of them. But you're safe, Charley; we've got you." A beetle darted out from behind a disturbed crate and scurried toward Sam's prone form, leaving a lacework pattern of tracks in the dust. Grace's small shoe shot forward, her toe crushing it with a quick pop.

Charley pushed away from her. "No! He isn't. He didn't. They boys are still here in the school. He was helping me."

"Charley, Sean's mother arrived this morning. He never made it home. They searched the school and the grounds, and they found his body in a garden shed, along with piles of bones. They found a hidden graveyard. The graves are small, full of only parts... Charley, I'm sorry. You have to trust me."

Charley shook his head, edging away down the hall. "It wasn't Sam. I saw Bowles. They never found his body on the moor. It was a box of rocks they buried. I was with him. Matron, they're all in the East Wing. I'm sure Sean's there, too."

"I know you thought him your friend. I'm sorry, Charley. Come with me to the headmaster. Speak for your friend, if you will, but let us show you the evidence—"

"Matron, where did you find that bottle?"

Grace looked at the bottle in her hand. Her eyes roved. "From my medicine chest, Charley."

"Sam!" Charley shouted at the gardener.

"Charley, no!"

"Sam, wake up!" The gardener stirred and groaned.

"Charley, quick! Get away from him." Matron Grace reached out for Charley, pinching his sleeve.

Charley pulled his arm from her grasp and ran toward the far wall, to the tunnel. He wasn't sure if he could move the planks at the bottom, wasn't sure if he could make it through the halls of the East Wing. He turned to the spindle ladder and began to climb, using his one good hand and his teeth clenched around the narrow rungs.

He heard shouting below and behind him.

He ducked his head and pushed at the roof access with his shoulders. The panel door swung up and flipped over.

Frigid evening air filled Charley's lungs. He stood in the opening, grasping at the slick stone tiles that layered over the wood boards of the roof. They sloped gently to long stone gutters, punctuated with pointing spires carved with vines. The grey stone flaked with age and lichen and centuries of rain and sun. The bell tower rose from the roof at the juncture of the four wings.

Charley felt the ladder shudder under his feet. He kicked himself through onto the roof and crawled toward the tower, the stone tiles leeching warmth from his fingers, numbing them.

He heard a voice behind him and looked over his shoulder. Matron Grace's face and shoulders appeared through the opening. "Charley, come back!" Her linen cap blew from her head and tumbled over the edge of the roof. She struggled, and pulled herself onto the tiles, staggering on her small black heels, arms outstretched for balance.

Sam's bloody brow appeared behind her, over the rim of the trapdoor. "Grace, leave him alone!"

Charley kept crawling, his left knee burning at the pressure of the cold, uneven tiles.

The matron screamed. Charley looked back. Sam had her by an ankle. She fell to the tiles, sliding across them. She kicked her foot, and Sam's grip slipped. She pulled her knees under herself and crawled over the slope, back toward Charley, Sam right behind.

Charley crawled faster. He reached the bell tower and straddled the ridgepole. Digging his right foot in, reaching with his arm, he gripped an outcropped stone on the carved face of the tower. He swung his left leg over and edged over the juncture to the roof of another wing.

Grace had reached the tower. She began to climb it, wrapping her fingers around the stone outcroppings. She scaled the carved vines and edged around the corner toward the wing where Charley rested. "I'm the only one who offered you a home, Charley—made you a home, a family."

"You hurt me!" Charley screamed into the wind.

"That's what families *do*," the matron growled.

Sam reached the juncture, below her. "Charley, come back this way! Give me your hand!"

Charley hesitated.

"Charley, I'll swing tha back round. You can go back through the trapdoor—go get help."

"Charley, don't!" Matron Grace screamed. She hooked her arm though a narrow window in the tower. Her apron flapped in the wind, the orange light of the setting sun shining through the crisp linen. She began to climb down the tower toward him.

Charley breathed. His gaze raced from the matron to Sam to the grounds far below. He felt again that sensation of falling: the plummet, breathtakingly rapid, yet all too slow. Forever in a moment. His head spun. He edged back toward the juncture.

Sam sat leaning against the tower, one arm hooked around its corner and the other outstretched to Charley.

Charley pressed his heels into the stones and reached. He couldn't touch the gardener's fingers.

The hem of the matron's apron brushed his cheek.

Charley stared into Sam's eyes. Sam nodded.

Charley kicked off the side of the tower. Sam reached. So did the matron.

CHAPTER THIRTEEN

Charley caught Sam's sleeve, and felt the firm forearm tensing as Sam's hand clamped around Charley's arm.

He screamed as pain raced through his injured arm. Matron Grace clung to his cast, the plaster shattering under her tight grip. Her fingertips dug into his twisted bone. Charley hung suspended over the deep slope of the rooftop juncture, where it funneled out to open air and the flagstones twenty meters below.

Matron Grace hung from his arm, kicking against the gutter by her heels. She pulled at him. Sam held on.

"I'm sorry for this, Charley—I'm so sorry," Sam said. Then he hauled on Charley's good arm, heaving him up higher onto the roof.

Charley's throat burned with the scream that tore from him.

The matron squeezed him. Charley looked down at her, blinking away the blur of tears and bright spots of pain.

"Charley, help me!" she called up at him, her face twisted in fear. She screamed and brought her other arm up, wrapping the hand around his limp forearm.

The gardener gripped him tighter, pulling with both hands, till he could wrap an arm under Charley's shoulder. "Let go, Grace! You're hurting him!" Charley heard Sam's teeth grind together, saw the scarred cords of his neck standing out in sharp relief.

Charley kicked out with his feet. He aimed for the matron's wrists. His vision was filling with white light, and he felt his face go numb under the freezing sweat, felt the pull of the dark tunnel. More of his cast crumbled away. The matron's fingers dug deeper into his arm. He kicked again, and one of her hands released its grip to grasp at his flailing ankle.

"Please, Charley! I'm not trying to hurt you. Help!"

Sam gave another heave. Charley felt Sam's other arm wrap around his chest and smelled the sour apples of his breath.

"Kick, Charley. Kick as hard as you can. I've got you."

Charley kicked. The matron screamed. Charley felt her fingers slip from his ankle, felt the weight of her transferred to his arm. He felt the black tunnel reaching up for him.

Her nails dug into the skin of his withered arm. He kicked again, hard, and felt the fingers release. He opened his eyes.

The matron slid down the angled slope of the roof. The heels of her black shoes caught in the gutter and she flipped over the edge, a screaming comet of white linen.

The scream stopped with a wet impact as the white spread to red on the flagstones below. Charley watched as the red soaked the white, as the apple voice told him not to look down and the strong arms pulled him back onto the ridge of the roof.

CHAPTER FOURTEEN

Charley felt small splinters puncture the bottoms of his feet as he staggered across the plank floor of the old attic. He clutched his injured arm to his chest, conscious of the unnatural movement under the skin, of the numbness spreading through his hand.

Sam pushed down on the hinged trapdoor, unfolding the ladder beneath him as it lowered.

"Be careful," Charley said. "Matron said that they think it was you. She said they're looking for you."

Sam paused, his foot on the top rung of the ladder. "If we hurry, we can get to th' headmaster's office while they're still distracted by…by the commotion. We can look for proof, then run for the village."

"We could use his phone to call for the police."

"I think the police are already here, Charley. Or at least on their way."

Charley nodded. "Byrne has letters—a stack of them, tied with a ribbon, hidden in a book with the key to his files. Maybe those could help us clear your name."

They descended the ladder. The servants' attic hall was empty, the rows of doors closed. They stepped light and quick down the hall to the service stairs that would lead them down to the first floor by the kitchens, where they could creep into the North Wing and to the headmaster's office.

They rounded the turns of the staircase. At the first floor, Sam slipped into the staff room and pulled a key down from the wall. They could hear the crowd behind them, at the front of the building where the matron had landed. There were shouts and heavy foot-falls, the jostle of a crowd moving toward the infirmary.

Charley peered around the main staircase and saw the still, red bundle of the matron's body carried between two masters. When the crowd disappeared behind the heavy door of the infirmary, Sam and Charley slipped out from behind the staircase and down the masters' hall to the tall double doors at the end.

Sam unlocked the door and they slipped inside, closing and locking it behind them. Charley raced to the bookshelf, sliding his finger over the tops of books until he felt the smooth panel of the box edge. He pulled it free and opened it, pulling out the thick bundle of letters.

The door handle rattled.

Charley shoved the box back in place and raced for the bedroom. He slid under the bed. Sam stood behind the bedroom door, press-ing himself against the wall next to the deep wardrobe.

The headmaster crashed through the office door and ran to his desk. Charley heard the chime of the phone.

"Please, send the physician from the village to the Old Cross School. Our matron is gravely injured—please tell him to hurry."

Charley had never heard his voice tremble before, all the sure-ness and arrogance stripped from it with the sharp edge of worry.

Headmaster Byrne slammed the phone back down and pulled the bottle from the drawer. He took a long, bubbling drag and walked into the bedchamber.

Charley watched Byrne's shoes, poking out from under the swaying black hem of his robe, cross the floor to the tall cabinet in the corner. There was a rustling noise, the sound of a lock releasing and the clamp of hollow metal.

"You bastard," the headmaster said.

The chamber door swung shut, and the dirty, worn boots of the gardener stepped forward, toe to toe with the polished black leather of the headmaster's.

"Will she live?" Sam asked.

"Not likely. You'll hang for this."

"Do they know that she's yours? Do they know what she's done? What you've both done?"

"What?" Byrne's voice tightened.

"She's your daughter, isn't she? And my half-sister," Sam said.

"Wherever did you hear such filth?"

"In the village, where tha sent me. An old woman who used to work here told me you were close to the earl's estranged daughter. So close she bore your disgrace and went mad." Sam's shoes advanced and Byrne's slid back.

"That's a filthy lie." Byrne's heavy whisky breath filled the room.

"Tell me, Byrne. Was she—my young mother—insane before she bore your child? What did tha do to her that she ran so far, gave it all up—even her own daughter? Your daughter."

"Shut up! I loved Eleanor. But I'll tell you, there were many men wondering if they were the ones who shared in her disgrace. I was the only one who loved her enough to share it, whether it was mine to share or not."

"Don't paint tha'sen so noble. Tha's covered her crimes here—you shared in those as well. Innocent boys have lost their lives."

"Is any boy innocent?" the headmaster spat. "Tell me, where is your little pet? You were seen on the roof. Did you throw him down, too?"

Sam lunged forward. There was a scuffle and a loud retort. The smell of cordite filled the air. Charley's ears rang.

Sam's knees appeared below the edge of the bed, then a hand soaked in blood. When the other hand appeared, a rain of red fell behind it. The elbows bent, and Sam's face appeared, pale behind dirt and dust, eyes grown dull and glassy like the film of a beetle's wing. His cheek settled to the floor.

Charley clawed at his throat to stop the scream that roiled there, building from the pit of his stomach.

Headmaster Byrne stepped into the spreading puddle by Sam. "Eleanor told me about you once, when she learned that you had lived. She said you fought her when she cut you. She said most boys looked shocked, or hopeful even, that her knife administered a cure and not a hurt. She said you never looked surprised. Not for an instant."

Sam's eyes rolled weakly. His lips moved, but a stream of blood came where words should have been.

"You've always known too much, it seems."

Charley saw the barrel of a revolver lower down by Sam's ear, and a shot rang out again, dulling the world white with sound and pain.

Charley squeezed his eyes shut against the warm spray that struck his face, and covered his ringing ears. He tasted blood on his lips. He sensed vibration on the floor, and his eyes shot open.

Headmaster Byrne strode out of the room, back to the phone. He picked up the receiver. "Police inspector, please... Inspector Tate, hello. Yes, the doctor should be here any moment. I'm calling with unfortunate business, I'm afraid. We've caught our man. He came at me in my chambers. I'm afraid I was forced to shoot him."

Charley's ears pulsed with the rapid beat of his heart. He stared into the hollow eyes of the gardener, at the gentle curve of his fingers on the floor, earthen island hills in a spreading sea of blood. *Sam.* Charley wanted to scream his name loud enough to bring him back. He couldn't even whisper it. *But I can clear it, Sam. I swear I'll clear your name.*

Charley clutched the letters. Correspondence between Ellie Forster and William Byrne. He slipped a thin sheet of paper from the bundle and unfolded it. He read of her relief at her father's death, about her misery in her new life, and that she would soon return to him and Grace. He slid the paper back in place and put the bundle in his shirt.

Byrne's shoes traversed the office carpet back and forth, and again, stomping fiercely. Charley watched the shallow ripple in the pool of blood at each heavy footfall. He ached to reach out to Sam, to hold his cooling hand. To whisper comfort to his ruined ear, a promise of a lifetime of prayers for his wounded soul. A promise for revenge.

The phone trilled, and the polished feet ran back to it. "Hello? Thank you, Inspector, yes, I would appreciate it if you would see to this personally. No, we haven't recovered any other bodies. Yes, I'm afraid the boy is still missing. The matron assured me he was recovering. Yes, the injured matron. I don't know yet if she'll make it." His voice broke. "We are awaiting the word of the village doctor. Yes, the gardener was seen throwing her from the rooftop. I understand there will need to be an investigation. Please do hurry. I'm afraid the dead man is in my bedchamber, where he'd been waiting for me. Thank you."

The phone clicked and the feet continued their pacing. They froze, and rushed back into the bedroom.

Charley covered his mouth with his mother's scarf, wrapping it two, three times, trying to stifle the panicked sobs creeping up through the hollow feeling in his chest.

The headmaster ran to the wardrobe and pulled it open, tossing aside folded clothes. He pulled out a long shelf and set it aside, then pushed at the back panel. It fell away, and he grasped the boards and pulled them clear. A light came on inside the hidden closet. Charley edged closer, peering out from under the bed.

A small brick-lined room lay hidden, recessed in the wall. It was full of guns and tins of food, and books. The glass eyes of a china doll peered from a back shelf, dark curls framing its delicate face. The headmaster gathered the books in an armful and carried them to the fireplace in the study, dumping them on the flickering hearth. When they were all removed, he replaced the panel and shelves, stuffed the disheveled clothes back in place, and hurried to the fireplace.

Byrne pulled a box of matches from his pocket and lit them, one after another, tossing them on the pile of books till it blazed. He threw the box of remaining matches on top.

He stood and brushed the dust from his robes, and left the room, locking the door behind him.

Charley slid out from under the bed and hurried to Sam's side, crawling through the cooling blood. He reached down and squeezed a strong shoulder. "Sam…" Charley's voice shook. He brushed wet hair back from the ruined forehead and held his hand in front of the still face. There was nothing left of Sam the gardener.

Charley stood. Every breath burned in his chest. He raced to the fireplace. The book covers were smoldering, their dry pages smoking and curling in the spreading fire. Charley grabbed a thick rug from the floor and threw it over them, stifling the flames. He pulled the books from the grate and batted out the tracing embers. He scanned the titles of the books, flipping through their burnt and browning pages. Surgical guides. Anatomical references. Instructions for the study of cadavers. Each inscribed with the names Eleanor Ward and Grace Byrne. Books guiding the curious hand, rather than the healing one—experimental, full of grisly illustrations and lacking any description of how to heal the wounds described.

He forced the hidden closet back open and replaced the books, propping the concealing panel loosely back in place—easily found by anyone searching the room. He walked to the desk and picked up the phone.

"Operator," came a woman's tinny voice, buzzing through the line.

"Police inspector, please." The line clicked and hummed, then another click.

"Inspector Tate, make it quick."

"If you're in a hurry to get to the school, there's something you should know first."

"Who is this?"

"Charley Winslow. I'm one of the missing boys. It wasn't Sam Forster that took me—it was Matron Grace. Byrne helped her, covered for her. Sam attacked the matron to rescue me, and then Byrne shot Sam." Charley lost his voice. He swallowed and tried to dredge it back up from his tight chest. "There are other boys there in the East Wing, where she kept us. They need help—please hurry!"

"Is this a hoax? Some sick joke?"

"No! I have letters, and books. Grace is the earl's missing grand-daughter—Byrne is her father. There's proof here, if you hurry! I was with Ethan Bowles when he died in the East Wing, from injuries given to him by the matron. Byrne lied to frame Sam."

"Stop! Quiet, now."

"I'm trying to help you!"

"Get back to your classes, son. Let the police handle this. Officers are on their way now. I'll be there myself shortly." Click.

Charley reached into his shirt and felt around for the key to the room. He let himself out the door and pulled it closed behind him, not bothering to lock it. He hurried down the hall. A mass of robes stepped out in front of him, and he crashed into it, yelping as his injured arm was bumped.

"Watch where you're—Charley?"

Charley staggered back, eyes and mouth agape. It was Master Crawley.

"Are you all right? The headmaster told us you were missing. We thought you were…that that man had—where have you been?"

"It wasn't Sam, Master Crawley, it was the matron and Byrne. Sam was trying to save me, and Byrne killed him." Charley began to shake; he could hardly keep upright. "We have to get the other boys out of the East Wing. Please, Master Crawley, help me get them out!"

Master Crawley put his hands on Charley's shoulders and steadied him. "Charley, are you serious?"

Charley sagged. Master Crawley caught him, then flinched back from the tacky blood that coated Charley's clothes.

"Charley…the East Wing is on fire."

CHAPTER FIFTEEN

The bell began to ring, long and loud, the continuous call that signaled everyone to the main hall.

Master Crawley looked down at Charley, at his battered arm and bloodied feet. "Come to my office, Charley. You'd best keep low till the inspector arrives."

Charley pulled away. "How can I trust you?"

"Charley—"

Charley ran. Throngs of students filed through the main hall, crowding the entryway, blocking all routes. Talk of the fire spread as quickly as flames.

"Does stone burn?"

"Told you this place is a death trap."

Charley stumbled into the infirmary. A circle of figures in black robes surrounded a bed with a mound of bloody cloth piled at the footboard. Low moans came from the center of the circle.

The doctor turned his head and saw Charley in the doorway.

"Charley!" he shouted and spun around. His sleeves were rolled up, arms bloody to the elbows, one of the matron's dark bottles in his hand. "We thought you'd been killed!"

"Doctor—many of those boys are still alive. They're trapped in the East Wing. We have to get them out of there."

"Charley, you're talking nonsense. The matron needs my attention now, or she may die."

"She's the one that locked us up, Doctor. Save her life so their mothers can see her hanged." Charley raced into the bedchamber off the infirmary. He tore aside the thin carpet and pulled at the floorboards till he found one that pulled free. He grabbed a candlestick from the bedside table, lit it, and lowered himself into the tunnel.

* * *

Another plank staircase stretched in front of him, steep and warped, cut deeply into the ground, lowering rapidly into another crumbling brick walkway with earthy walls. The wood planks of the stairs were spattered with old stains, a patina of dark splotches. Alcoves in the walls held stacks of bones: a cross-hatch of arms, a pyramid of skulls.

Charley's bare feet grazed across the loose crumbs of brick dust. He sheltered the candle close to his chest, by his wounded arm. The twisted flesh didn't feel the heat.

The tunnel shot straight several hundred meters to another staircase. Charley climbed. At the top, he set the candle down and raised his arm to the boards, shoving the planks out of place. They gave aside, and he climbed up through the floor of the dark twin infirmary chamber. Charley glanced at the shoes visible beneath the curtain hem. He rounded the tattered curtain and stared into the shrunken membranes of her eyes, the pale leather of her face, her hands gnarled in her lap. He ripped down the bloody curtain of aprons and threw it over her. He grasped the back of her chair and dragged it to the hole in the floor. Her head trembled stiffly on her dry neck as he dragged the chair, banging down the wooden stairs and into the tunnel.

A dozen meters back into the darkness, he shoved the chair to the side and ran around it, back into the East Wing. If the place burned, he hoped she'd remain as some evidence left unspoiled.

There was no sign of smoke in the infirmary, nor any sign of the mad, wounded boys.

Charley squeezed his eyes shut. He was one of them, he knew. This was his school, his family, now. A community of peers. He was the new twisted boy of the East Wing, and he would shuffle these boys back into the light. He ripped the crumbled remains of his cast from his numb arm and dropped the tattered gauze strips to the floor. The flesh of his arm was darker than before, bruised and twisted. The bloody stumps of his missing fingers swelled. Charley wiped the plaster dust from his hand into his hair, powdering it white.

"Hello?" he shouted, the sound of his voice was absorbed by the curtains of cobweb. There was no answer.

The infirmary door was unlocked. He pushed through and ran to the servants' stairs. As he climbed, the air grew hazier, stinging his eyes.

The second-floor hallway was deserted, the row of doors flung open to filthy dormitories. The twisted boy's body was gone, the trail of his dragged corpse sweeping through the dust on the floor. Ethan was gone, too. The third floor was empty; the stink of the rooms was cut with the growing scent of smoke.

A loud pounding came from above Charley's head.

Heavy planks covered the entry to the stairs leading to the servants' attic. Shiny new nails stuck deep into the peeling, varnished doorframe.

Charley ran back to the second floor and into the inner-wall passage. He hurled himself up the stairs to the long attic room.

The wall beside him banged and rattled as he climbed, the air filling with smoke. He wrapped his mother's scarf around his mouth and nose.

The long attic eaves sweltered like an oven. Weak light fought through the smoke to stab at the darkness, illuminating the hanging oddities. Heaps of toys and crates were thrown around the room, smoldering, the flames creeping through dusty old dolls and shrunken birds, climbing up the heavy beams to the rafters. The weakening roof planks groaned under the weight of the stone tiles.

Charley ran down the length of the room, dodging small fires that ate through the abandoned tack boxes full of lost boys' treasures.

The roof snowed ash as he reached the end of the room. The reeking mattress was set aflame, the fire racing up the partition wall beside it. Charley gripped the corner of the mattress and pulled. He kicked aside the charred table. There, in the corner, lay the remains of a folded ladder, the trapdoor tied with thick rope to a ceiling beam. Charley nearly wept with relief.

He pulled a surgical saw from the shelf and hacked at the rope till it gave. He knelt, leaning his weight against the hinged door, unfolding the rusty ladder into the dark, smoke-filled space below.

Scarred hands reached into the glow of flames, grasping at the cracked wood of the ladder. Charley reached his hand down through the floor.

A sea of eyes, glinting in the firelight, shone back along the central hall of what had been the servants' quarters. They moaned and coughed, shuffling toward the ladder, pressing up against it.

"Charley?" A voice came from the crowd.

"Sean?"

"Charley, run!" Sean shouted from somewhere in the dark smoke.

"I have to get you all out," Charley shouted back.

"They won't thank you, Charley—don't let them catch you!"

He felt fingers graze his outstretched wrist, then the sharp edge of a broken tooth. Charley gasped and choked on the thick smoke. He pulled back, standing over the hole. He forced his lungs still and shouted down into the space, "Matron is dead, or nearly. She can't hurt any of you anymore!"

"She's been dead for years—that's never stopped her," Sean bellowed. "This is *her* school. These are *her* students."

"No, the other matron—her daughter—you're safe from her now, but you need to get out!"

They were surging up the ladder. A hand grasped his knee, hauling at him, pulling itself up. Charley's leg buckled. He felt fingernails rake his scalp, fingers twisting in his hair. He scrambled back, felt his hair slide through their desperate grip, ripping from his scalp. He fell back. Fire licked at the back of his neck. He lunged to his feet.

Arms grew like tendrils from the hole in the floor as twisted boys pulled themselves over one another out of the trapdoor. Charley heard moans and screams, muffled under the weight of boys.

Charley ran. Stone tiles crashed, raining around him as he wove through the climbing fires. His lungs fought, screaming for air in the thickening smoke. He plunged through the wall into the stairway and threw himself forward, willing his feet to match the speed of his descent.

A thundering of feet followed from above as he stumbled through the wall at the second floor. He ran to the servants' stairs, around and around. Steps echoed his own, gaining, as he raced to the infirmary.

He jumped down into the hole in the chamber floor, his toes gripping the edges of stairs, launching over the old brick. His feet caught. His arm whipped forward and wrapped around the pliant husk of the dead matron as he fell over her, rolling across the tunnel floor, her long dry hair tangling around his face.

Charley kicked at her, tugging free, choking on the dry rot smell that covered him, clinging like dust to his clothes. He scrambled to his feet, clutching his arm, the pain splintering anew through the battered flesh.

In his fall, he'd lost his direction. Sounds seemed to come from all around, pounding overhead. He reached out with his feet and felt the dry frame of the old chair. He made a guess and ran to the right.

He slammed into a soft mound of flesh and bounced backward, his head cracking against the bricks of the floor.

He heard a click. A bang. Bright flash, ringing ears, brick fragments exploding against the side of his face, carving new wounds.

"I don't owe you this mercy, Charley. Better to leave you to the fire. But I'm anxious to end this trouble."

Charley scrambled back as another flash lit the tunnel, the bullet burying itself in the wall, spraying clumps of clay. Byrne advanced.

Charley flattened himself against the tunnel wall. He could hear the sweep of Byrne's foot as he felt in front of him, heard the polished shoe catch on the dead matron.

A rapid staccato of bright flashes followed as Byrne, thinking he'd cornered Charley at last, fired bullets into the body of his old lover. In the light from the muzzle flash, Charley saw tiers of shining eyes advancing through the darkness down the hall.

Charley turned and ran past Byrne.

Behind him, Byrne cried out. His gun fired again, twice, before it clicked uselessly in the darkness.

Charley slammed his feet up the plank stairs as Byrne's screams punctuated the agitated moans of the pain-maddened boys whose mothers he'd lied to, whose tack boxes he'd pushed away into shadows, whose files he'd burned.

Charley pulled himself up through the floor. He pushed the planks back in place and drew the carpet over them. He pulled at the edge of a tall cupboard and tipped it over onto the trapdoor, spilling its contents across the room.

Men in suits rushed over, filling the doorway. They stared at Charley.

He became conscious of the blood running from his scalp, the burnt tatters of his clothes, the stinging cuts on his face and feet. Of the stiffness in his arm, which had begun to swell again, hanging limp at his side, bulging purple at the wrist and elbow.

Charley stared back, at the bright metal shield pinned to the vest pocket of the man at the front.

"Inspector Tate?" He stepped forward, trembling. The floor pounded below him, the cabinet jumping from the impact.

Charley fainted. He felt many hands catch him, slowing his fall to the rattling floor.

CHAPTER SIXTEEN

Charley breathed deep, drawing in the smell of apples again and again, as if filtering their nourishment through the clear air. He peeled back his eyelids and scanned the room for Sam, for the source of the apple scent. Sunlight fractured through a collection of jars clustered on a table by his head. Small black bodies crowded within them, scurrying and fluttering, reflecting bright iridescent light from their carapaces.

Charley watched the spindle legs dance in the light and breathed in the apples. He drifted in and out, watching the light change, till the jars glowed orange.

Solid footfalls on the floor made him turn his head. The doctor's grey beard came into view, stark against the black of his jacket.

"It's good to see you awake, Charley. How are you feeling?"

Charley croaked, stretching his voice. It felt as though the East Wing fire lived in his chest. "Did they get them out?"

The doctor sat in a spindly chair that squeaked, sending a shock through Charley's skull.

"The police did recover seven boys from the tunnel below the school. They have been moved to a hospital in London to recover—mind and body."

Only seven. Charley sighed.

"The bodies of Master Byrne and an older woman, who had been dead some time, were also recovered. They are still searching the remainder of the East Wing, and have found a number of…" The doctor pulled his glasses from his nose and polished them with the hem of his coat.

"The twisted boys," Charley said, "the lost boys the matrons took." He strained his shoulder to lift his left arm. Nothing happened.

The doctor pinched his nose, eyes squeezed shut. "I've been here a dozen times and never saw…never thought…"

Charley reached with his right arm, felt along the side of his body, working up to the wrapped stump at his shoulder. His hand trembled over the rough bandages.

"I'm so sorry, Charley," the doctor said.

Charley's breath came ragged. "I understand, Doctor." Heat spread across his temples. "Where am I?"

"In the carriage house, where Sam Forster lived. I understand that you were friends, and I didn't feel it was best for you to stay in the infirmary."

"Thank you," Charley said. He felt his eyes heat and spill over. He nodded to the collection of jars. "Where did they come from?"

"Many were already here in the house. Your head boy Malcolm brought a few more."

Charley smiled. "So they all know. What happened, I mean—that it wasn't Sam?"

"I believe they are putting together the pieces, yes. It will be a while, I fear, before it all becomes clear."

"Doctor, what about Grace?"

"She has survived, so far, though she has lost both legs at the knee. She speaks nonsense, mostly, but there are things she says that show she was, at least in some way, aware of what had been happening behind the walls of the school. She asks repeatedly for a Benjamin, which happens to be the name of the first boy to disappear. We believe his body was among those recovered from the East Wing."

"The boy with the backward leg."

"Yes."

"He was the one who took us. Who brought us to her. He's the ghost that the boys talk about, that the teachers won't."

"There is some evidence, in the debris, that they grew up together in that attic. His leg broken so he couldn't flee—his mind broken too, after a time. As were the others."

"I was with Ethan Bowles when he died," Charley said. "He was sleeping. It was quiet."

"I am glad for his sake, Charley, that he found peace. There's not much left of those boys locked away in London. We were fooled, Charley. I should have seen it years ago, but Byrne is an old friend. Was one. I never thought him capable of—"

"What will happen to the school?"

"It has been shut down. Master Brown has sent the students home."

"Home? Will I go back to my father, back to Cairo?" Charley raised his head, leaning up from the pillows.

"That's unlikely, Charley. Your father's base is no place for a boy in these times. There are other schools taking on students, and families warding the children of soldiers. Don't worry, Charley. We'll find you a place."

* * *

Charley walked across the frozen grass, snapping the tender stalks, pulling the leathery skin from a dry winter apple with his teeth. The wind blew up behind him, creeping beneath his tattered linen scarf and collar. The stitches in his cheek pulled as he stretched his jaw to bite the apple. The trees above him rattled empty branches.

Scaffolds surrounded the East Wing, pulleys and cranes arching over it, lowering piles of burned slate tiles that had folded into the attic space. Every so often, a platform was lowered, carrying a figure wrapped in a white sheet. These figures lay lined up in the grass, while the crane rose again for more.

The doctor had said a dozen boys had come out in white sheets. Charley had asked after Sean, but the doctor said it was impossible to say. The bodies taken from what had been the attic no longer had identities.

Charley watched two village men dig at the turnip patch, the only ground soft enough in the winter grass, now a small cemetery for the lost boys.

Charley clamped the apple in his teeth. He knelt on the frozen ground and lowered a canvas bag from his shoulder. He pulled a row of jars from it, and gripped them in his knees as he unscrewed the lids, setting the jars back down in the grass on their sides. Small shining bodies darted from the glass enclosures, and vanished into the tall dry grass of the orchard.

He brushed aside dark leaves lined with frost. Here was a soft patch of turned earth, where the gardener had dug for insects. Charley pushed his thumb into the dirt, shoving it aside, feeling it press deep into the creases under his fingernail. He picked away at the frozen ground till he found a soft spot and hollowed it out.

He pulled the apple core from his mouth and pushed it into the hole, sweeping the earth back over it and patting it down in place, to take root.

Sarah Read is a dark fiction writer living in northeast Wisconsin with two sons, two cats, and a husband. She's a librarian in a castle on an island in a river where she specializes in children's and teen programming. Her work can be found in Ellen Datlow's *The Best Horror of the Year Volume 10, Black Static, Suspended in Dusk volumes I* and *II*, among other places.

You can keep up with her work at inkwellmonster.wordpress.com or on Twitter or Instagram @inkwellmonster.